CHIN MUSIC PRESS
1501 Pike Place #329
Seattle, WA 98101-1542
www.chinmusicpress.com

Chin Music Press is based in the traditional territory of the Coast Salish
People, the Duwamish (dxʷdəwʔabš), in land that touches the shared
ancestral waters of the Suquamish (dxʷsəq́ʷəb), Tulalip (dxʷliləp), and
Muckleshoot (bəqəlšuɫ) Nations. We honor the people past, present,
and future who belong to this place.

Cover image: Grand opening party at the Davenport Hotel, Spokane,
Washington, 1914. Courtesy Northwest Museum of Arts and Culture/
Eastern Washington State Historical Society, Spokane, Washington.
Charles Libby Photograph Collection. Photographer: Charles Libby.
Image no. L87-1.265.

First Edition
Printed in Canada

ISBN paperback: 978-1-63405-053-1
Library of Congress Control Number: 2022930081

Book and cover design by Cristen Crujido

THE STRANGE BEAUTIFUL

CARLA CRUJIDO

CHIN MUSIC
PRESS

For my mom, Deanna, and my son, Kai.

Do not ask questions of fairy tales.
Jewish Proverb

Contents

Prelude: The Apartment Building

Welcome to Mt. Vernon Apartments. Beyond these doors lay over a century of stories. Stories that have soaked into my walls, saturated my floorboards. Been tucked into closets and corners and cupboards. Set atop radiators and windowsills. Stories overlooked, stories forgotten. Everyday stories of everyday people who have lived under my roof, my watchful eye. But as we all know, the everyday often holds hands with the magical and the extraordinary. Some insist I am enchanted; others claim, a portal to the past. A few say, I draw those to me who need a place for their magic to dwell. I say yes to all. Don't believe me? Choose an apartment–I have ten–suspend your disbelief, listen to the story it has to tell.

Apartment A: The Songbird
(1918)

S hell shock is what the doctors called the incessant humming in Thomas's ears, his brain. But he had no words to describe what had happened to his left eye, his left cheekbone, the scar that mapped the left side of his face. The doctors pretended that once he returned stateside his life would right itself. *A hero's welcome*, they said. He found no such reception when he got off the train at the Great Northern Depot in Spokane, Washington. In fact, there was no one there to greet him at all.

The platform was eerily empty, save a few porters; inside the station was a poster issued by the US Army meant as a reminder to returning soldiers: "Behave Yourselves." As if the bloody battlefields had stripped the men of all humanity. Thomas looked up at the north face of the four-sided clock, its hands twinned at twelve. He pulled his cap down over the gaping hole where his eye had once been, and his mask up to the bridge of his nose. In the dark, if he kept his head down and his mask up, he might be mistaken for whole. Normal.

Thomas's parents had succumbed to the death wave they were calling the Spanish Flu—first his mother, then his father—while he was being put back together in a Paris hospital. Celestina, the girl who had begged him to stay faithful, begged him for a ring, told him she had wed a cowboy from Montana and would be making her new life in Wolf Point. "Do not," she wrote, "come looking for me." He took this to mean: I cannot love half a man.

Thomas had no home to return to, so he walked under the elevated tracks, block after block, until he found himself on First Avenue at the front door of the Willard Hotel. He asked the clerk for a room for the week. The man barely looked up from his newspaper. He took Thomas's money, pushed the key across the desk, and pointed to the stairs. "Fourth floor, Madison Street side," the man said, then went back to reading. The room was small (an iron bed, a dresser, a sink) but clean. Thomas shed his cap and coat and went down the hall to use the toilet and wash off the grime of travel. When he settled back into his room, his stomach roiled with hunger, and the war voices began their nightly ghost opera.

It had been two years since Thomas last walked these streets, and with the epidemic came a curfew. But Thomas knew he was a man who people had stopped seeing once he'd lost the dark beauty that had defined him. Under the cover of night, he became even more invisible. He put his cap and coat back on and headed toward Chinatown. On Front Street, he battled a bearish wind coming off the river. As he pulled open the door to the restaurant, rain thrashed and thunder roared.

He took the last booth in the shotgun room and sat facing the kitchen, his empty eye socket to the wall. He pulled his cap from his head and ran his fingers through his hair. The waiter came to his table with a pot of tea and set a small white cup in front of him.

"Chow mein," Thomas said without looking up.

He drank his tea and ate the noodles slick with oil and heat, as fast as he could. He'd lost his eye patch on the train between Chicago and Spokane, and he was self-conscious of the hole in his face. A little boy on the train, who was studying him over the seat, asked, "Is you a pirate?" Before Thomas could answer, the mother grabbed the boy and pulled him back into his seat. "Shame on you. How rude!" she said. But Thomas didn't mind. At least the boy looked at him as if he were a human being, unlike the adults who stared and turned away in horror. He speared the last sauce-soaked water chestnut on his plate as a group of men came in and sat behind him.

"The Davenport Hotel is looking for men," he heard one say. "Stop in and talk to—" He didn't catch the man's name because the waiter stopped at his table to leave the check. Thomas handed him a dollar bill. "Keep the change," he said. Then he bolted the rest of his tepid tea, secured his mask, flipped up the collar of his jacket, and stepped out the door into the rain.

The next morning, Thomas walked to Joyner's Drug Store, where he bought a new eye patch and a Hershey bar. He ate the chocolate, one rectangle at a time, as he walked up Lincoln to Sprague to the Davenport Hotel. As he stood under the elaborate metalwork marquee, he thought of the night he proposed to Celestina, on one knee, in the middle of the hotel's restaurant. He thought, too, of the night he celebrated the hotel's grand opening with the city's movers and shakers. Invited because he was having a clandestine affair with one of the shakers. *A lifetime ago,* he said to himself, before pushing through the revolving door into the lobby. At the front desk, he pulled off his cap.

"Can you direct me to the man in charge of hiring?" asked Thomas. The clerk looked him over and winced. "I most certainly cannot," he said, with an edge that sliced—swift and deep. Thomas's patch slipped, revealing his empty eye socket, exposing more of the angry scar. The man gasped. "Sir, the guests!"

Thomas repositioned the patch, pulled the brim of his cap down as far as he could, and turned to leave. He once had a face that drew men and women to him; their compliments fueled him, kept him hard, kept him moving through life with his eyes forward, his ego stroked. None cared about the books he'd read, the poems he'd written, the songs he'd played on the piano. People only saw his face, the way his body moved under his clothes. Now when he looked in the mirror, he no longer saw the man he was, only the monster he had become.

"Sir?" He kept walking, his cheeks a conflagration. "Sir!" He stopped and found himself looking directly into the saucer eyes of the small, russet-haired young woman from the front desk. The rest of her face, from the bridge of her freckled nose down, was obscured by a mask.

"Miss Fine," she said, extending her hand. "I apologize, some people can be so insensitive. Follow me and I'll take you to Mr. Stevens's office."

Miss Fine escorted Thomas to a small reception area, where a secretary asked him to be seated. As Miss Fine turned to leave, Thomas said, "Thank you. I owe you one."

"Buy me a Coke sometime, and we'll call it even," she replied. He could see she was smiling by the way her eyes flickered. She turned to leave and then turned back around. "Do you have a place to stay?"

"I have a room," he said. "At an SRO down the street."

She walked over to the desk, picked up a pencil, and scribbled a phone number on a piece of paper. "Call my sister. She manages an apartment building on the South Hill and is looking for a caretaker." He nodded and thanked her again. The secretary reappeared. "Mr. Stevens will see you now."

Thomas left the interview with a job and a renewed sense

of hope. "Report back at 4 p.m. tomorrow," the man said. Before he left the hotel, Thomas slipped into a phone booth in the lobby to call Miss Fine's sister, Mrs. Ward.

"Meet me at Mt. Vernon Apartments in one hour," the woman said.

He took the streetcar up the hill and walked the remaining cobblestone blocks past Craftsmans and Revivals and an occasional Queen Anne (all painted rainy-day tints of gray and blue) to the corner of Tenth and Adams. Mt. Vernon Apartments was unlike anything else on the street. It was Colonial, red-bricked and white-pillared, three-storied and balconied, its wide lawn ornamented with boxwood and maple trees. It was billed, Miss Fine had said, as "Spokane's Most Modern Apartment." She also used the words high-class and splendid, and mentioned a garage in the back—one stall for each apartment, each with its own entrance (which told Thomas the tenants could afford to own automobiles).

Waiting at the top of the concrete steps, under the portico, was a woman with fox-red hair, a green velvet coat, and a gauze mask peeking out from under a scarf. Glamorous.

"Mr. Baldassarre." The woman extended her gold-gloved hand, but Thomas noticed that she flinched when he took it.

"Mrs. Ward," he said. "A pleasure."

She unlocked the main door and, as he followed her from floor to floor, recounted a list of duties she expected him to perform as caretaker. As she spoke, he realized the job was his, and he let go of the fear that she would say no because of his ravaged face. To Thomas, the building whispered opulence with its flocked, midnight wallpaper, sea-storm wool carpet, and Arabian tapestries holding vigil on each landing. Like Mrs. Ward, the building was boldly elegant. She took him to the attic and pushed open the door to the apartment that would be his.

"Mr. Baldassarre, welcome to your new home."

Five nights a week, he reported to the Silver department in the basement of the hotel. His job: to wash and polish the silver coins before they were given back to the guests as change. It was a service that the owner, Mr. Davenport, felt set the hotel apart. It was a job that Thomas was happy to have, but he still found the idea of it amusing. His parents would have found the humor in it, too, if they were still alive, this marriage of their professions. His father had made his money in the copper mines of Butte; his mother worked in the laundry of the Thornton Hotel.

On the nights that Thomas worked at the Davenport, he was so exhausted that he fell into a deep and silent sleep. On his nights off, he found himself half dreaming, half remembering the carnage of war: the rivers of blood thick and wide, the smell of spent explosives and raw meat, the men calling for their mothers as they lay dying. He'd wake fevered, wet with sweat. His head pounded, his heart beat out of his chest. Come morning, he would get up and take a deep pull of whiskey from the bottle he kept under his bed, though he knew the liquor would only get him dressed and out the door. Silencing the demons that had taken up residence inside of him, halting the visions, required something stronger. The streetcars didn't run late at night, so he'd take a taxi to the edge of Chinatown and walk the rest of the way. No need for anyone to know exactly where he was headed, not even the men who drove cabs after midnight. Thomas liked this four-block neighborhood that never slept—the constant jostle of bodies and the cacophony of voices (Chinese, Japanese, German, Italian, Greek), the smell of joss sticks and river fish, cooking oil and cigarette smoke. It made him feel more human, less spectral. The door to the opium den stood between the noodle joint and the fan-tan parlor. Once inside, it would be thirteen steps down to sweet oblivion. A pull from the pipe, and the dragon would swallow him. In a state of half-lucidity, he would dream himself whole.

However, the harsh reality of morning would strip him of this fantasy. He would take the streetcar back to the apartment, and make a plate of eggs and sourdough toast. A pot of cowboy coffee, bitter and harsh. The rest of the day he'd spend unclogging drains, letting the milkman and grocery delivery boys into the apartment's back door, and tending to the complaints of the tenants. In the hour between one job and the other, he would soak in the tub, smoke, read, and listen to records on the gramophone.

Late one December night, Miss Fine stopped Thomas as he was returning from a cigarette break. She placed a hand on his arm.

"You're here late," he said.

"There was a party," she said. He didn't ask her what kind of a party, and she didn't offer any information. Christmas, he remembered. Uninvited, he thought.

"I have a favor to ask," Miss Fine said. "We lost a bellman to the flu. The one who took care of the fish and the songbirds. Would you take over until we find someone new?"

"For you, Miss Fine, anything." A strawberry blush rose to her cheeks.

"Please," she said, "call me Margaret."

At midnight, he left the kitchen and walked up the staircase to the lobby. He opened the first of the cages. *Clean, feed, water, cover,* Margaret had reminded. The songbirds chittered in conversation. The sound was unexpected, shrill.

"I won't hurt you," he said. He pulled the paper from the

bottom of the cage. It smelled of shit and piss and blood, and reminded him of the animal smell of the battlefield. He poured bubbling liquid into crystal bowls, dipped his finger in, and tasted it. Champagne. He filled gold-edged pink dessert plates with triangles of coconut cake. Strange, but he was not paid to ask questions. Before he closed the cage door, a bird landed on his hand and trilled in a pitch so high it was a shriek. Had he injured it while moving half-blindly around the cage? He tilted his head to get a closer look. It wasn't a bird at all, but a tiny winged woman in a silk gown: onyx black hair, skin as pale as spilled milk, eyes of blue. She sang out. It sounded like a plea. He bent and flashed the light around the cage. It was filled with tiny winged women in tiny silk gowns. The one in his hand sang out again and again.

"I can't understand you," he said, as he leaned in. She took a deep breath, her voice slowed, deepened. "Save me!" she sang. He closed his fingers around her and slipped her into the pocket of his work shirt, carried her there until he could hide her in his locker in the break room.

"I have one more hour here, and then I will come back for you. Do you understand?" She nodded. He held up his finger. "One hour," he repeated.

He moved in a rhythm from cage to cage, feeding the tiny winged women. Then he went downstairs to the men's room to feed the fish. He flipped open the top of the aquarium that filled the entire north wall. A fish floated at the top of the tank. Dead. He scooped up its wilted body and walked to the nearest stall. He turned the net upside down, but the fish stuck to it. He pulled it from the netting, held it in his palm, touched the black back of it. It felt like wet wool. He flipped it over and saw that it was a tiny man in a tiny tuxedo. He dropped the man into the toilet and flushed. How many times had he passed the aquarium or the birdcages and not noticed what they held? *People see what they want to see*, his mother used to say.

Thomas uncapped the bottle marked FISH and sniffed. It smelled of juniper berries, gin. The men rose to the surface and opened their mouths while he poured. He took the postage stamps of French bread from the brown paper bag and scattered them across the top of the water. Then he walked down the hall to the employee locker room, where he tucked the tiny woman into his jacket pocket. On Sprague, he hailed a taxi. He put his hand into his pocket and held the tiny woman, a palmful of silk and feathers, all the way up the hill.

In the morning, he searched the garage until he found a tarnished birdcage in the rafters. Tenants moved and left pieces of their lives behind. These remnants, he had been instructed, were to be stored away in case the people returned. He knew none would. He cleaned the cage and hung it in front of the window that faced the alley.

The tiny woman learned to slow her speech so he could understand her words. She told him her name was Avi, told him how she was captured, how she came to be at the hotel.

"In a meadow, high in the Selkirk Mountains, there is a pond with small swimming men and trees with tiny winged women. At the beginning of every summer, a short, bald, barrel-chested man used to come and steal us. To prepare his capture, he would sprinkle whiskey-soaked crumbs of vanilla cake on the ground and then wait for us to flock. He knew we loved cake, couldn't resist its intoxicating thrill. Then he would strip off his clothes and ease himself into the pond, pleasure himself, and cover those closest to him in his stick. Afterwards, he'd scoop up the small swimming men and put them in pickling jars filled with pond water. Pluck the cake-drunk, laconic winged women off the ground, and toss them into his fishing bag. If there weren't enough of us, he would pull out his butterfly net and capture those trying to escape him. Then he would take us to the hotel and sell us to his brother. The one whose night duties you took over."

Before Thomas left for work the next day, he put Avi in her cage and closed the curtains to the neighbors' prying eyes. "Nap," he said. When he came home, he made them both a midnight dinner of baked beans and brown bread—then, she sang him to sleep. The next morning, he read the paper out loud over milky coffee and toast with huckleberry jam. She perched on the table next to his plate to eat and drink.

Winter sewed itself into spring, and the horror of the epidemic started to wane. Thomas no longer visited the opium den on Trent or the brothel on Howard. He no longer felt shattered by sadness.

On mornings when the sun was out, Thomas would take Avi to the roof. He would drink coffee and read the newspaper, while she flew around him in circles. When he would rake the yard or touch up the paint on the apartment's outer walls, he'd set her cage in the grass under one of the maple trees lining the property. She'd sing along to the music she heard floating from an open window above. It was always Puccini.

Thomas and Avi cultivated a husband-and-wife routine. He cooked for her, heated water for her teacup baths, cut articles from magazines, and taught her to read. With the torn tips of flower petals, she applied salve to his scars. She told him stories—real and imagined. She made him laugh. They learned to make love to each other. She fluttered over his closed eye, his sharp cheekbone, his lips, his chest, his torso. She sang songbird songs as she moved down his body. Flapped her wings against him until he was hard. Then faster and faster until she was exhausted, and he was spent. She pressed her breasts and pelvis into the hair of his stomach. Rubbed against the tip of his finger until she peaked. Other times, he slipped a silk ribbon between her legs, moved it back and forth until she sang with joy.

"Beautiful," they said to the other. He was happy and so was she.

The men in his department noticed his newfound confidence. How he sang as he worked, joined in when they joked.

"A woman," they said. "Deserved," they also said.

One April Sunday, Thomas and Avi spent the afternoon on the roof. They drank black tea and ate white cake. Avi sang arias to him in Italian; he read poetry to her in French. He planted a profusion of flowers for her: pansies, petunias, peonies. He placed her cage in the center of the roof garden, but she preferred to sit on his thigh. Afternoon slipped quickly into evening.

"Hungry?" he asked.

"Always," she sang.

"I'll go to Chinatown and get us dinner. You want to stay here on the roof?"

"Yes! The light is so lovely. I want to bask naked in it until you get back." She laughed. It was a trill of G notes.

Thomas hummed one of Avi's favorite songs as he walked from

the streetcar to the restaurant. He took a seat at the counter. "Let me guess," the owner said. "Egg rolls and chow mein?"

Thomas smiled and handed over his metal lunch pail. "Wife's favorite," Thomas said. He dropped sugar cubes into his tea and read while he waited. Fifteen minutes later, Mr. Kee set the dinner-laden lunch pail on the counter.

"Next time, bring your wife and I'll make you a special dinner. Family recipes."

Thomas thanked him and laughed at the thought as he walked into the gloaming.

Thomas was three steps out the door when he was slammed into the wall by a policeman. On the sidewalk, his book lay trampled and spine-broken, his dinner scattered. Men to his left and right from the opium den, old comrades in pain, all equally molested.

"Let me go," he said. But that just got him turned around, cuffed, and led to the police wagon with the men from the raid.

Avi's cage swayed in the wind, the sky darkened.

"Thomas?" she cried. "Thomas, where are you?"

The wind whipped and frothed. It pulled Avi up and pushed her down—over and over again. By the time she grabbed hold of the cage door, her hands were raw, her arms, legs, and breasts lacerated, one wing bent, the other broken. *Hold on,* she told herself. *He'll be home soon.* It became a prayer. The thunder clouds gathered overhead. She looked through the strands of hair plastered across her forehead, her eyes. "No," she whimpered, then started to cry. Lightning silvered the sky. "One, two, three," she counted. Did not make it to four, before there was a crack of thunder. She cried harder. There was nowhere to hide. A crow arrived on a gust of wind—blown and disarranged. It eyed her though the cage. "Leave me alone," she sobbed, as it moved closer.

Thomas didn't sleep. The rain assailed, the thunder shattered. Is she safe? The thought became a scratch on a record—skipping and repeating, skipping and repeating.

Thomas's bail was posted on Monday afternoon. Margaret waited for him at the bottom of the courthouse steps.

"Thank you," he said, as he pulled her into a hug. "You're the best friend a man could ask for."

"Thomas?" His name was a question. She looked as if she might cry.

"What?" he said.

"Nothing," she said, instead of what she really wanted to say—which was, *I love you.*

"I have to go," he said.

He ran in the direction of the apartment, toward Avi. Finally, he stopped and hailed a taxi.

"Where ya goin', Mac?" the driver asked.

"Tenth and Adams. Drive as fast as you can."

Ten minutes later, the cab pulled up in front of the apartment building. Thomas threw two dollars over the seat, ran to the front door, fumbled with the lock, and raced up the stairs to the roof.

"Avi! I'm here," he called out. "I'm home." As he got closer, he saw a black hillock on the bottom of the cage. A crow—on its back, its eyes open. "Avi!" he cried. He pulled the crow from the cage and saw the pale pink moons of her nails peeking from under its bedraggled feathers. He lifted its wing and there she was—naked, white as eiderdown, lips eggshell-blue, marked with blood—sheltered but breathless. He had done this to her. He had killed her. His tears doused her storm-matted hair, ran over the blood on her skin. He grabbed the heads of the pink peonies from the pot nearest him and laid them at the bottom of the cage. He rested Avi on top of them, placed the crow next to her, and carried them to the apartment.

Thomas awoke at 4:00 p.m. the next day, and took the streetcar downtown to explain his false arrest to Mr. Stevens and ask for time off to collect himself.

When the secretary saw Thomas, her smile turned to a scowl. "He's not available," she said, and returned to the typing he had interrupted. Thomas walked past her and opened the door to the office—without permission, without knocking.

"Mr. Stevens," he said.

The man looked up, his face hard. "Who allowed you in here?"

"Mr. Stevens," Thomas repeated.

"I was told you didn't clock in last night, nor did you tell anyone of your whereabouts. That, Mr. Baldassarre, is grounds for dismissal."

"Let me explain," said Thomas.

"Judging by the look and smell of you, you have not bathed or combed your hair. The hotel prides itself on the appearance of its employees. We have standards, Mr. Baldassarre. Standards!"

"Sir—"

"Go," he said pointing to the door. "Or I will be forced to call security."

Thomas stepped forward, leaned over the desk. He took in the starch of the man's collar, the slick of his hair, the cleanness of him—soap and aftershave. Without a mask covering the lower half of his face, Thomas could see the straight thin line of his lips, the droplets of sweat forming above them.

"Now," Mr. Stevens said. His voice squeaked, as he gave his final command.

The animal smell of Thomas started to rise: the unbrushed tang of his breath, his unwashed armpits, the sharp metallic edge of blood. He pressed his palms into the wood of the desk, to keep from putting them around Mr. Stevens's neck. He wanted to squeeze it until the man lost his breath, until his eyes popped out. Instead, he took Stevens's face in his hands, kissed his mouth, walked out the door, and closed it behind him.

"Good afternoon, Mr. Baldassare," the elevator operator said, smiling at Thomas.

"The basement, Miss Smith." She turned the lever and the doors closed. Normally chatty, she remained silent as she watched him in the polished brass of the elevator doors.

"Mr. Baldassare," she said, "you look—" she stopped.

He ran his fingers through tangled hair, over his ruined face. "I know," he said.

He entered the men's restroom, stepped up to the aquarium, flipped open the lid. The small swimming men saw him and rose to the surface—expecting bread, expecting gin. He pulled the men from the tank, three at a time, five. Threw them onto the floor and watched as they gasped and writhed. He twisted his boot onto those not yet dead, until they exploded. Then he took the back stairwell to the lobby, where he opened cage after cage. He seized tiny winged woman after tiny winged woman, and crushed each one in the unforgiving, repetitive clench of his fist. He threw others against the wall and watched as they fell, bloodied and dying.

Thomas left the hotel and ran down Sprague across Lincoln to Monroe. He stood in the middle of the bridge and looked east over the city that loved and vilified him. He climbed onto the wall and felt the late afternoon sun on his face. Then he raised his arms over his head and dived headfirst into the Spokane River. She opened her arms and accepted him. Whole.

Interlude: Thomas and Avi

If you ever find yourself walking across the Monroe Street Bridge at sunset, stop and watch as the sun casts its goodbye glow over the city. Look down toward the slate swirl of the river. See anything? Look a little harder. There on the south bank of the river. See it now? Your eyes aren't playing tricks on you, it's him, her—Thomas and Avi—shrouded in river mist and song.

Apartment B: The Tower
(1918)

Because it is 1918. Because there is a flu called Spanish. Because you are delicate. Your lover keeps you locked in your third-story apartment to keep you safe.

"A damsel in a tower," he says as he runs his fingers over your unbrushed hair.

He brings news of Spokane to you, but only tells you the things that won't make you think worrisome thoughts. He bakes you complicated cakes and pretty petits fours. He dotes, cajoles, worships, smothers.

At the beginning of the epidemic, you rouge your lips, braid your hair, dress in Chinese silk pajamas—jade for day, ivory for evening. It feels like a novelty. Soon you switch to cotton union suits the color of dirty bathwater, let your white-blonde roots go dark, stop braiding your hair, stop wearing color on your lips, stop looking in the mirror.

The days accordion into each other, each exactly the same as the one before: wake; drink coffee; eat toast; wash dishes; take a bath; brush your teeth and your hair; read; eat chocolate; nap; listen to records on the gramophone; eat a quarter of your lover's steak, a sliver of cake, drink half a glass of basement-pressed red wine; wash dishes; sleep. Make love every other day, and always on Sunday.

You weren't always this dull, didn't always feel this morose, this useless, this lethargic—but being inside, all day, every day has taken its toll. You stare at the same four walls for hours on end. If you walk into another room, you see four new walls. The sameness of each day steals you from yourself.

You used to be wildly irreverent, daring, unconventional, a mad flirt. In the life you lived before the epidemic, you were a photographer in Seattle. You worked for Asahel Curtis in his studio in the basement of the Stuart Building. Made lantern slides of the city: its buildings, streets, people. You went to art lectures and political rallies; slept with painters, poets, and labor organizers; drank too much gin.

You came to Spokane to photograph the city. Mr. Curtis booked you a room at the Davenport Hotel. "Elegant," you telegraphed. After dinner, you wandered the hotel's halls, walked its staircases. You took photos of songbirds in cages, women manning the elevators, gilded mirrors holding sentry at the end of hallways, beautiful people crowding beautiful rooms. You peeked into a party in the Marie Antoinette Room and saw that dessert was being served.

The sugar embraced you, the butter invited you to stay. You smoothed your dress, straightened your spine, lifted the tipped end of your Scandinavian nose a little higher in the air. You found an empty seat and excused yourself to the table for being late—a lie, but you will do anything for sugar. A waiter placed a slice of cake in front of you: a staircase of marzipan, cake, custard, cream, and jam. It was pink, green, white—royal. You ate it quickly, asked the waiter for another slice for everyone at the table. The women nodded, the men laughed. "Please," they all said.

The baker was called.

"If a man ever makes me feel the way your cake does," you said, "I'm marrying him." He smiled and thanked you, then returned to the kitchen, leaving you and the table of sugar-drunk revelers to return to your merrymaking.

The next night, there was a wedding in the Hall of Doges. You spied the baker and waved. He motioned for you to wait. He disappeared and then returned with a slice of cake and a glass of champagne. He put his finger to his lips when you asked where the champagne, now forbidden, came from. Then asked, "Dinner? Tomorrow?" You looked at the cake, the perfect waves of pearlescent frosting; the champagne, its gold-white bubbles rising to the surface of your glass. He was not someone you could see yourself seducing, but what he did with sugar, butter, and vanilla turned you on. In his hands they became holy.

"Okay," you said.

"Meet me in the lobby at seven."

You lifted the cake from the plate and took a bite. Your knees buckled with the pleasure of it.

"Tomorrow," you said as you walked away.

It was the end of you, singular, and the beginning of you, plural.

The flu hits the city hard. Spokane closes on a Tuesday: schools, theaters, movie houses, churches. Weddings are banned, funerals; cigar-shop poker games are too. On Wednesday, the first death is reported. The news of two hundred deaths follows on Thursday. Halloween is canceled. Spitting is illegal. Wearing masks is law.

Besides your lover, the only person you see now is the apartment's caretaker, Thomas. His war-damaged face, a beautiful ruin. You wave to him from your window, mouth a silent *hello*. Besides your lover, the only person you talk to now isn't a person at all. It's a crow who sits on the neighbor's roof directly across from your bedroom window. You talk, it answers. It talks, you listen.

Your lover says Spokane is empty, haunted.

"I want to see it," you say. "Photograph it."

"It's not safe," he warns.

"I'm lonely," you say. "I miss my life."

"How can you be lonely?" he asks. "You have me. Your life is with me now."

You nod and bite the inside of your lip. Do not tell him the only thing keeping you in Spokane is the epidemic. Do not tell him that a life devoid of laughter is lonelier than being alone. Do not tell him that treating you like a caged songbird isn't love. Do not tell him he does not feel like home.

You go out to the garage. Pull down a box from your long-ago life. A life your lover wants you to erase, to forget. Inside, you find a goodbye gift from an unrequited crush. A man you could not conquer. It is an art magazine from Berlin—an issue dedicated to Marc Chagall.

"I saw his work in Paris," he told you. "It reminded me of you—radical, otherworldly, fanciful. Women flying away from men. Men flying away from women." He moved his hands through the air to illustrate his point. "Untethered by the prosaic and the pedestrian. Just like you."

In your memory he is young, while you are growing older. You understand that time is unfair, unjust. You tear the image of a woman floating away from a man from the magazine, take it upstairs, and tape it to your vanity mirror. Every time you look at it, you wonder what happened to the *you* he saw.

One Friday morning, after your lover leaves for work, you triangle a scarf and tie it over your face. Your reflection is a Wild West bandit, a bank robber. You walk to the streetcar and take it downtown. No one is allowed to stand or hold the strap or lean into one another, everyone must face forward, everyone must wear a mask. You get off the streetcar at First and Lincoln. A strange stillness shrouds the city. The streets are close to empty, and you think of Pioneer Square after midnight—the place and hour you miss the most. You point your camera, first at the twin stacks of the Steam Plant, and then, at the Lion Hotel, now a temporary hospital to house the indigent, the flu's worst cases. Here, death is visible—it dances in the windows and on the roof. You see a nurse standing near the hotel's front entrance. Purple bruises of exhaustion half-moon her eyes.

"May I take your photograph?" you ask. She nods.

You thank her and smile, then remember your mask. You aren't sure your smile reaches your eyes. You move quickly away from the reality of the plague playing out beyond the hotel's walls, the flu's victims on stretchers draped with white. Your hunger for a downtown escapade now feels reckless. Dangerous. You are shaken, ready to go back up the hill. Fear has stripped you of your boredom and bravado. You put your head down and walk as fast as you can toward the streetcar. A hand on your arm stops you.

"What are you doing here?" It's your lover. "Have you

lost your mind?" he asks. His eyes are bulging—a marriage of anger and fear.

"Why aren't you at work?" you ask. He holds up a box from the Crescent Department Store in answer. A present, you realize, for you.

"I'm going mad," you say. "I had to get out."

"Don't you understand?" He takes you by the shoulders and looks into your eyes. "You could die. And then," he says pointedly, "I would be alone." The strangeness of his comment flutters, drops, splatters on the sidewalk. The extreme nature of his adoration suddenly makes sense. It sickens you. You are his plaster against loneliness, the chronic aloneness of bachelorhood. He takes you by the arm and pulls you toward the car.

"Let me go," you say.

"I'm taking you home," he says. He pushes you into the passenger's seat. Drives you silently up the hill. You are a child being punished. The next morning, he goes to the hardware store and buys three locks. One for the front door, one for the back, one for the window that opens to the fire escape.

"What are you doing?" you ask.

"Making sure you don't get out again."

One week knits into three, three into five. You write long letters to the short list of people you miss the most. You ask your lover to bring you something alive to love. You imagine a cat, black and mystical, or a poodle with clouds of curls. He brings you a jade plant that you unimaginatively name Jade. You carry it from room to room and talk to it. Like the crow, the plant becomes a friend—the keeper of your secrets, your dark thoughts. The flu bullies the city. Your lover worries that he will lose his job. He brings home his woes, pours them over you, crushes you under their weight. His worry wakes him at two, at four, at six. He tosses and turns, gets out of bed, and paces the long hallway of your apartment. You wake each time. Are exhausted by seven, before your day even begins. You do not love your lover the way you wish you could, but you do not want him to be felled by sorrow. You try to lift his spirits, try to make him laugh.

"Let's drink whiskey," you say. "Dance." You pull him toward you by the waistband of his trousers, throw your head back and laugh.

"Don't be ridiculous," he says. "We have nothing to celebrate."

"We're alive," you say. "Isn't that the best reason of all?"

"Enough," he says, and he pushes you away, leaves you standing in the middle of the living room.

You have forgotten why you said yes to your lover. Agreed to live with him here in a city not your own, far from family and friends. You remember only that after a string of unkind men, his adoration astonished, his attention delighted. Normalcy felt like an adventure. He does not make your heart skip beats. Does not make you laugh. Barely speaks to you. *Why, you ask yourself, did you give up your life for this?* Why becomes an endless echo.

You yearn for deep discussions about the quiet culture of aesthetics. Your lover does not read, does not worship at the altar of art. When you introduce topics that interest and excite you, a look of disdain flashes across his face. Is followed by, "What are you talking about?"

As an act of personal protest, you utter a single word for seven straight days, varied only by your intonation: "Oh. Oh? Oh!" The only *oh* to garner a reaction is the flat one. To which he replies, "Oh, what?" His question deluged with disgust. You are flummoxed that he doesn't notice the change, then furious.

You crave sex, hot and dirty. Your lover is lean, muscled, exceptional for his age, now leaning into forty, but the sex is as dull as his wit. He presses his closed lips to yours, presses you into the sheet, into the mattress. You want to melt, drip, be licked—instead, you are pressed. He is Victorian in a modern era. He is, you realize, a prude.

Your loneliness becomes an extra appendage. You strap it

down, hide it, pretend you are happy, pretend you love him.

As your sadness grows, you start to float. At first you are an inch off the floor, then three. Soon you drift from room to room—your shins hit the kitchen counter, the bathroom sink. You hold onto furniture to moor yourself. Eventually, you spend entire days pinned to the ceiling.

Your lover does not lose his job. Instead of working less, he works more. Fearful of the flu, two-thirds of his staff quits. He leaves every morning before nine. Is gone for ten hours, eleven—works six days a week, sometimes seven. When he comes home at night, he brings dinner from the hotel. Always steak, medium rare; a baked potato, buttered and salted; a slice of cake, chocolate. You eat in silence at the dining room table. The only conversation, the scrape of a knife, the shriek of a fork.

The weeks hopscotch from November to December. It's Tuesday. Your lover is working late, making cakes for the holiday season—stacked, filled, frosted, fancy. In spite of the danger, people continue to celebrate. A misguided nod to normalcy. Your lover bakes their cakes, the hotel pretends not to notice their parties.

You put a record on the gramophone, Puccini's *La Bohème*.

Take your red silk pajamas out of the drawer—from a shop on King Street in Seattle's Chinatown, from your life before. Before you moved in with your lover, before the flu, before you were sugared with sadness. You sit in front of the mirror, braid your hair, crisscross it over the top of your head, pin it into place. The moon strokes you with her long fingers of light. You paint your lips red. It shocks after a string of colorless weeks. You spritz perfume on your throat, your wrists. You study your reflection, wish someone else could see you painted and dressed. You open a bottle of champagne and drink it straight from the bottle—the pop and fizz of the bubbles enliven you. The music's notes knock against the glass. You open the window to a rush of snow-frosted air. The aria invites you to follow its crescendo out the open window. You and the music float out over the city. Away from your lover, away from the apartment, away from the sadness. Away, away, away.

Interlude: The Lover

On the night she floats out the window, her lover comes home to an empty apartment, an open window, the gramophone needle skipping in the record's final groove—the sound repeating and repeating and repeating.

Apartment C: The Mannequin
(1934)

"**P**erfect," the window dresser says as she slips the shoes onto the mannequin's delicately arched feet. She ties the laces into tiny bows, slides the box stamped *Made in Italy for the Crescent Department Store* across the floor, and checks her watch. It's nearly seven. Tomorrow, she will take the mannequin down to its new home in the Dress Salon; tonight, she's late for dinner with Angela, the Italian beauty from Cosmetics. She turns off the overhead lights and closes the door to the workroom.

As soon as the window dresser walks out the door, a jolt zigzags from the arch of the mannequin's left foot to her right, then lightnings up her body where it ends at the tip of her nose with a sneeze.

"Excuse me," the mannequin says to no one. She takes a tentative step forward, wobbles slightly on the curved heels of her shoes, leans forward, and peers at herself in the mirror. In the waning half-light of the room, it's hard to make out the details of her reflection, but what she sees she likes: dark hair, braided and coiled at her ears; gray, almond-shaped eyes; high, sculpted cheekbones; a narrow nose; a serious mouth. She is small-breasted and narrow-hipped. Modern.

She finds a pencil and pad of paper on the work table, wants to leave the window dresser a note so she does not worry. *Thank you for the shoes*, she writes. She stops, taps the pencil against her upper lip, looks around the room, and sees an empty crate, on the end a single word in bold black. This she takes as her name and signs the note with a flourish—Manikin.

The next morning, when the window dresser arrives in the workroom, the first thing she notices is the empty space. Who could have taken her mannequin at this early hour? Hers! She bets it was her coworker, Martin, or as she calls him—the department do-gooder. There was a rumor (that she did not start, but loved to spread) that he had a hand in his predecessor's quick departure the season before she started working at the store, and she believes it. He is so perfect, so fake. Never a hair out of place, his clothes always impeccable. He reminds her of a matinee idol. She hates going to the movies (such a waste of time) and she hates Martin. If not Martin, maybe it was Sal. The one who reminds her of Angela, with his coffee-brown hair and eyes. A face from a country with a sea and endless sunshine; a body built by manual labor that creates waves of whispers from the salesgirls, and the men, on all six floors. He calls her *baby*, and wants to unpack the crates he delivers to her from the warehouse, wants to help her assemble the mannequins and move them around the store. Sometimes she lets him, just to watch the way his muscles move. If she liked men, she would choose one like him. A specimen, she thinks, and then laughs at the thought.

She sets her lunch pail and thermos on the worktable and notices a note written in perfect cursive. She is alone on the floor, alone in the store except for the night watchman downstairs. No one at this hour hears her scream. She leaves the store without explanation—she does not return.

The window dresser was wrong about being the only other person in the Crescent, besides the night watchman. Manikin is still trying to find a way out of the store. After she leaves the workroom, she takes the employee staircase down to the sixth floor, and then the elevator to the first. When she sees the watchman dozing by the employee entrance, she gets back in the elevator and goes to the second floor. In Luggage, she selects an ivory suitcase and then moves through the dimly lit store, filling the case with things she will need for her new life: slips and panties, garters and silk stockings, dresses and blouses and skirts. She sits in a chair until the sun rises and spills across the floor. The clock above reads half past seven, two more hours until the store opens and she can make her escape.

At nine o'clock, she goes back downstairs. She checks on the watchman, who is now awake and still at his post by the employee entrance. She sneaks over to Cosmetics, and regards her reflection in the morning light. Runs her fingers over the remnants of plaster in the dip of her throat, between her breasts, the nape of her neck. She plucks a compact of powder from the top of the case to camouflage the uneven spots, a tin of mascara to draw people's eyes to her own. As she kneels to pull lipstick from the bottom shelf, she hears the plaster crackle in the crooks of her elbows and knees, and then a swell of voices. The employees are arriving. She moves toward the Hat Bar, dons a cloche, and pretends to be what she was only hours before—a mannequin.

When everyone has gone upstairs to clock in, she picks up the suitcase and walks quickly toward the door. As she steps outside, she runs into a besuited, bespectacled man. She hits him in the shin with her suitcase.

"My apologies, sir," she says. "I didn't see you."

"None the worse for wear, miss," he says. He looks at the suitcase and then at her.

"I thought—" he starts. Then extends his hand. "Mr. Paterson. I'm the manager here at the Crescent. You must be Miss Clementine Barman. A surprise I must say." He shakes her hand so vigorously she is afraid it will come off. "Your telegraph letting us know you were turning down the position was disappointing, but I'm happy you've changed your mind."

"Sir," she says, but he interrupts her and continues.

"If you'll follow me back inside, I will have my secretary book a room for you at the Davenport Hotel until we can find new living arrangements for you. The apartment we reserved at the Espanola was taken by the new menswear buyer." He leans forward and pushes the button for the elevator. "We have connections all over the city, I'm sure it won't take long to find something else." He keeps up his one-sided conversation as she follows him to his office. During the elevator ride she learns that she—or rather, Clementine Barman—is from Portland, worked for Meier & Frank Department Store, and is the new head buyer of womenswear for the Crescent.

Clementine spends the next two weeks settling into life in Spokane. She eats her breakfast in the hotel's Delicacy Shop (a cheese Danish and a cup of coffee), a snack in the Coffee Shop (a seltzer and a cheese sandwich), dinner in the Apple Bower (English pea soup and strawberry shortcake). She has her hair washed and set into waves in the Beauty Salon; her nails filed into tapered points and painted with a sheen of polish. A *tint*, the manicurist calls it. Clementine buys a dozen dark red dahlias at the Flower Shop for the desk in her room; a stack of movie magazines from the Newsstand; a box of chocolates from the Confectionary. On the first night of her new life, she stays up until a yolky light floods her room—the candy box empty, the paper wrappers strewn on the floor, the magazines read.

"Charge everything to your room," Mr. Paterson had instructed. He also handed her an envelope filled with cash for incidentals and said, "Go have a bit of fun, dear girl, before your life becomes the store."

She walks up and down the streets of the city's main shopping thoroughfare, and discovers all sorts of new-to-her places: the imported shoes at Schulein's, the diamonds in the window of Dodson's, everything paper at Graham's, and a necklace of other stores that call to her: drugstores and dime stores, soda fountains and candy shops.

The second week, she moves into a furnished luxury apartment at Mt. Vernon. The building is Colonial, pillared, three-storied. Her apartment is up thirteen steps, through two sets of double doors, and after one gilded birdcage elevator ride to the third floor.

"Fancy," she says to the manager, as she takes in the oak finishes and built-in sideboard filled with crystal and porcelain, the contrasting modern furniture. All Danish.

"Lucky me," she says.

"I'd say," he says, as he hands her the keys to the apartment.

After he leaves, she walks from room to room. There are six. The vanity and moon-round mirror in one of the bedrooms invites her in. She sits on the velveteen cushion of the brass stool and studies her reflection, runs her fingers over the remaining bits of plaster in the dip of her throat, the nape of her neck. How did she go from a mannequin to this? A real woman, with a real life.

On her second day of work, Clementine is waved over to a cafeteria table by a woman she recognizes from the Cosmetics department.

"Join us," the woman says.

Clementine sets down her tray and introduces herself.

"Angela," the woman says. Angela is a mesmerizing swell of lips and hips and breasts and hair—a Verdi opera of a woman.

"And this," she says, pointing in turn to each woman at the table, "is Katherine, Opal, Marie, and Bettina."

"You all look like starlets," says Clementine.

"Not in the morning, we don't," Angela laughs.

"Speak for yourself," says Bettina as she pushes a wave of hair out of her eyes.

"Opal is telling us about her spring nuptials," says Angela.

Clementine listens as Opal talks nonstop about her dress, the where and when of her wedding, her future children, dog, house with a white picket fence.

Angela interrupts Opal. "What about you, Clementine?"

"I'd like a dog," she says.

Bettina takes the interruption to turn her attention to Clementine. "So, what's your story, morning glory?"

"Story?" Clementine needles with fear. She has no story

to tell. Bettina lights a cigarette, and blows the smoke across the table. "Where did you grow up? What does your father do? Do you have any brothers or sisters? Are you married?" All innocent but impossible to answer questions, except the last one.

"No, I've never—"

"Met the right one?" Angela finishes. "If you ask me, there is no right one. Men!" she laughs. "An absolute filthy bunch. Except that one," she says, pointing across the room.

"Martin!" she calls out. He walks over to the table.

"Ladies," he says, his eyes landing on Clementine. When the women notice him not noticing them, they resume their conversation on matters of matrimony.

Martin puts his hand on Angela's shoulder and asks, "Have you heard from Kate?"

"Medical Lake," she says. Angela turns to Clementine. "The sanatorium," she also says, answering Clementine's unasked question.

"How are you holding up?" Martin asks. Clementine sees Angela run her finger over her lips, as if to say *quiet*.

"Darling, have you two met?" Angela asks, changing the subject.

"Not yet," says Martin and smiles. Clementine notices the way his brown eyes flash green and crinkle at the corners. Angela introduces them. He is movie-star handsome: dark brilliantined hair, dark eyes, a thin mustache. He is dashing, debonaire. Tall, but not too tall; slim, but not too slim. He extends his hand. Clementine takes it and feels lightning jolt through her. The same feeling she had the night she came to life.

"Clementine," he says.

"Martin," she says. She holds onto his hand until she hears Bettina laugh and say, "Ridiculous." Embarrassed, Clementine pulls her hand back, upsets her cup. Coffee splashes onto the front of her dress. Embarrassed anew, she excuses herself, picks up her tray, and walks hurriedly away from the table.

"Who is that enchanting creature?" she hears Martin say.

"That, my dear, is your future wife." Angela's velvet laugh follows Clementine out of the cafeteria and down the hall.

After lunch, she realizes she must create a history for herself and fast. There is only one way to do it. She buzzes her secretary and asks her to buy a round-trip train ticket to Portland. "Make sure it's on the Columbia River Express," says Clementine.

On Saturday morning, Clementine packs an overnight case and catches the 7:15 out of the station. She opens the magazine she bought at the newsstand and absentmindedly flips through the pages until she arrives at an article titled, "How to Behave Like a Lady." She reads it once and then again. It is filled with an exhausting list of *do nots*. Ladies do not talk too loudly or too much. Ladies do not drink from a bottle. Ladies do not drink beer. Ladies do not drink too much. Ladies do not swear. Ladies do not wear bright red lipstick. Ladies do not apply lipstick in public. Ladies do not chew gum (lest they look like a cow chewing cud). Ladies do not discuss religion or politics (or any subject that might offend). Ladies do not speak of private matters publicly. Ladies do not reveal their secrets. The *do nots* match the rhythmic chug of the train: ladies do not, ladies do not, ladies do not. There are so many rules, how can she remember all of them? Will being a woman ever get easier? she wonders. She tosses the magazine aside and stares out the window for the rest of the trip. The train passes through flaxen fields of wheat, over and along the wild Columbia River, with its basalt walls climbing up and away from the shoreline. She sees a highway trace the tree line, stands of pine so thick she can't see between them, the shock of a waterfall cleaving the scene in two, and then, a crown of a building atop a hill. Her train veers south. Finally, she arrives at Portland's Union Station. The porter accompanies her to the taxi stand and asks her where she is going. She only knows one place in this city.

"Meier & Frank," she says.

The taxi deposits her in front of the sky-scraping, sugar-white shopping emporium. She stands on the sidewalk and admires the grandeur of it. Her coworker, Sigrid, told her that Clark

Gable once worked here selling ties. Ties! Imagine walking into the store and being waited on by the future movie star.

"Move it, dolly!" a man says as he pushes past her.

Clementine picks up her case and walks into the store. It is a wash of ivory and black, metal and glass. It is elegant, refined. She studies the store directory. Fifteen floors and only two hours to cover them. Her first stop, the Coffee Shop on the tenth floor for a cream-cheese sandwich and a cup of coffee; then a peek into the Georgian Room (ladies eating late lunches) and the Men's Grill (no women allowed). From there she goes quickly from floor to floor, department to department, until she arrives on the third floor: Women's Apparel. It was here that she worked as a buyer in her make-believe life. She pulls a pocket diary from her clutch and pencils notes for the new old life she has to create for herself. As she moves through each department (Day, Evening, Resort, Bridal, Furs); she studies the displays (wool suits and satin gowns—all trimmed or topped with fur: mink, sable, ermine, fox); peeks at price tags (expensive, but lovely); looks at what the salesgirls are wearing (black afternoon dresses are all the rage); and glances into the eyes of the mannequins, searching for a sparkle of life (she sees nothing).

The closing bell rings as the elevator deposits her back on the main floor. Clementine looks up at the clock hanging above the display cases. It's almost half past five. She walks to the candy counter, buys a box of Alisky caramels, and asks for directions to the nearest hotel. The woman wraps her purchase and directs her to the Imperial.

"A four-minute walk," she says. "A right, a left, and a right. The name is on the stonework above the entrance, you can't miss it."

At the hotel, she studies the map she bought at the train station and the city directory borrowed from the front desk. She learns the city's streets and shops, its neighborhoods and businesses. She outlines the fiction of her past.

By the time she gets back on the train, she has a tale to tell. How her father was a dry goods merchant with a shop in Portland's commercial district, and it was over plates of noodles at the Republic Cafe that she learned the retail trade from him. How she grew up in a house on 5th and F. How she started working at Meier & Frank as a salesgirl when she graduated from high school, and worked her way up to a womenswear buyer. How Friday nights were spent with her mama and papa and two sisters (both younger), lighting candles and saying prayers over braided bread, and then walking to temple for services after dinner (this she borrowed from a conversation she overheard on the train). How she has never been married, but was once engaged. Even if her history is fabricated, feeling connected to someplace and a string of someones makes her feel less alone in the world.

After Portland, her days pleat into each other: a taxi to work, phone calls to vendors in New York and Chicago, walking the sales floor to see what women are wearing. She spends hours poring over budgets and sales reports. She has lunch with Martin and the Cosmetics clique in the cafeteria, except on Wednesdays, when she goes to the Tea Room to watch the lunchtime fashion show. She attends a circus of afternoon meetings and takes a taxi home to have dinner—alone. She has almost forgotten the beginnings of her new life in this city. It's only when she feels a tiny crack in the remaining circle of plaster at the nape of her neck that she remembers.

As she fingers the plaster spot, she thinks of the first time a man approached her on the sales floor and asked her a question that shocked her speechless: "What are you?" he'd asked. The second and third time she was asked, she pretended that she heard her name being called and excused herself. It wasn't until a woman posed the question in the elevator—and there was no escaping her or it—that she found the nerve to ask a question of her own. "What do you mean?" she asked, her brow furrowed.

"You're so exotic," the woman said, "I was wondering where you are from."

"Portland," Clementine said.

The lady laughed, "Before that, dear."

Clementine remembered the crate she'd arrived in.
"Berlin," she answered. The woman nodded, satisfied with
Clementine's response. It was after this encounter that
Clementine understood people's inclination to point out
another's differences, whether it was well-intentioned or not.

One Thursday, Martin stops her on her way out the door
after work.

"A matinee on Saturday?" he says.

"I thought you'd never ask," she says.

At one o'clock on Saturday afternoon Martin pulls up in a
green Franklin convertible, looking silver-screen handsome.
The sky is slate and cloud-stitched; the top of the car,
Clementine notes thankfully, is up. She leans over the balcony
and waves at Martin.

"Be right down," she calls. She checks her lipstick in the
mirror and smooths the front of her new blue Hattie Carnegie
dress. This is the third date of her life, but the first that she is
excited about. Her first was with Fred, the menswear buyer,
who took her to the Italian Gardens at the Davenport and
before they were done with their spaghetti asked if she'd like
to get a room upstairs; the second was with Lyle from Sporting
Goods, a man who spoke only of his predictions for the 1934
football season, and smelled of a curiously vile combination

of cedarwood and Limburger cheese. He took her to Bob's Chili Parlor for dinner. She liked the chili, she liked the tamale; she did not like Lyle. But Martin was different. He was unassuming, intelligent, mannered. He smelled of grapefruit and vetiver and freshly laundered shirts. When she tried to buy them coffee from Johnston "The Coffee Man" or hot doughnuts, fresh from the fryer at the next shop over, he never let her pay. "Because he's a true gentleman," Angela said when she told her. "One of the rare ones."

Their date is a mashup up of fun: the new Charlie Chan picture at the Fox Theater, two towering slices of chocolate-frosted cake and four cups of black coffee at The Percolator, then a stop at Krohl's Market after Martin offers to make her dinner.

When they get back to her apartment, the front rooms are frigid. She's forgotten to close the balcony door.

"You turn on the radiator, and I'll start dinner," says Martin. A look flashes across her face that must read as fear, because he suggests, on second thought, that she find something for them to listen to on the radio. She admits that she is scared to turn on the radiator, scared to light her stove, scared to start a fire—she does not tell him why. She defaults to damsel, but she's terrified that the fire or the steam heat could disfigure or destroy her.

Clementine drinks the martini that Martin mixes and watches

as he moves expertly around her small galley kitchen. When dinner is ready, they sit on the davenport in front of the unlit fireplace, and he pours them each another martini from the shaker. He lifts his glass to hers. "Prost!"

"You're German?" she says, instead of toasting.

"Direct from Berlin," Martin says and laughs.

"Me too," she says. "I mean—"

"I know," he says.

She takes a bite of the cheeseburger, closes her eyes, and hums as she chews, savoring the salt of the meat, the tang of the cheese. Martin laughs. "Good?"

"Where did you learn to make food like this?"

"Angela taught me," he says, reaching out to wipe the mustard from her chin.

"Oh," Clementine says, disappointment darkens her voice. "She'd make a perfect wife, don't you think?"

"For someone, but I'm not exactly her type."

"But you two seem perfect for each other." He gives her a funny look. "You think so?"

"Absolutely," she says and takes another sip of her drink.

"Whatever you say, kid." He reaches over and musses her hair, almost touches the plaster spot at the nape of her neck. She jumps off the davenport, alarmed. "You need to go," she says.

He laughs and then looks at her. Confusion in his eyes.

"You're serious?"

"Dead. Go." She points to the door.

"Got it," he says. He sets his martini glass on the table, puts his hands in the air—a Wild West cowboy—backs away from the davenport. She hands him his coat and opens the door. In the hallway, he turns. "I apologize for upsetting you." She stares at him, unsure of what to say. He pushes the button for the elevator, and she closes the door without saying goodbye.

After he leaves, she pulls the wool blanket off the back of the davenport, wraps it around her shoulders, and goes out onto the balcony. She hears music floating across the hall from her neighbor's apartment. Puccini's *La Bohème*. It is the only record he listens to, night after night, from as soon as he gets home from work until he goes to sleep at exactly midnight. His loneliness is a resounding crescendo. She wonders if hers has a sound as well?

The sky loses its stitching and the rain clatters over the cobblestones on Tenth Avenue. Clementine is soothed by its metallic melody. She's mortified by how she acted—but what if Martin knew the real reason she asked him to leave? What would he say then?

Clementine avoids the cafeteria and Martin for the next week. She eats alone in her office or doesn't eat at all. She ducks behind displays when she sees him; she arrives at the

63

store early and leaves late. But after a week of hiding, she's exhausted by her own efforts. On Monday morning, she leans into the half-open door of the workroom and knocks on the doorframe, then she walks in and sets a pink bakery box on the worktable. Martin opens it, pulls out the plum Danish, takes a bite.

"I accept," he says.

"My lunch invitation?" she says and smiles.

"That too," he says and laughs.

After that, the two fall into a pattern of spending their lunch hours together—eating grilled cheese sandwiches at the Woolworth's counter, sharing a Reuben at Nim's, or getting noodles from Luzon Café and eating them in the workroom. Clementine's and Martin's coworkers begin to comment, kindly and unkindly, on their pairing.

"Made for each other," they overhear the coterie of salesgirls in the cafeteria say.

"Made for each other is right," a man at their table adds. "They think they're better than the rest of us."

"Shut up, Stanley," says one of the girls. "You're positively green."

Soon the race toward Christmas is under way. The holiday catalogs have been shipped, the windows dressed, the mannequins outfitted. Toyland is frosted and flocked and waiting for children's Christmas wishes to be whispered to Santa.

One morning, Clementine gets a call from the warehouse that the order of Claire McCardell dinner suits she expects from New York has been lost in transit.

"Lost?" she shouts into the receiver. "Lost? How can you lose an entire shipment of dresses?" The man on the other end stutters an excuse. She slams down the receiver, clips her earring back on, slips on her coat, and storms out of the office.

She walks quickly down Riverside toward Lincoln, toward an argument. As she nears the Crescent's warehouse, she sees a man standing in front of the building smoking a cigarette. She's seen him in the store, but he has never acknowledged her in any way. She smiles as she passes him, says *hello*.

"I know who you are," he says.

She stops and turns around. "Excuse me?"

"You heard me." He drops his cigarette and crushes it into the sidewalk. "You walk around the store thinking you're someone important, but I know exactly who you are."

"I don't know what you are talking about," she says. She turns and walks as fast as she can toward the Crescent's wholesale office building. As she opens the front door, she hears him call out a string of numbers. It is the serial number stamped on her left hip.

After this, the man haunts her days. She sees him in the store and on the sidewalk after work; once, he is standing across the street from her apartment building, smoking a cigarette, and staring up at her third-floor balcony. How long will it be before he spills her secret? Before he tries to destroy her?

She carries her worry with her for over a week and finally tells Martin how the man from the warehouse is stalking her. She has never seen Martin angry, but a cherry hue rises to his cheeks, and the coffee he is drinking sloshes over the rim of the cup and soaks the cuff of his starched, white shirt. She tells him how the man stares at her, feels ever present. How she is scared to be alone at work, or at home, or in-between.

"Starting Monday," Martin says, "I am picking you up and taking you home each day."

"I can't ask you to do that."

"You didn't," he says. "End of discussion."

On Saturday morning, Martin arrives at her apartment with a present—a poodle. It is a cloud of white curls, one eye ringed in black, the other in pink.

"I can't be here to protect you," he says. "But he will be."

"Does he have a name?" she asks. He winces and laughs, "He answers to Pipsqueak."

She calls him Pip. He follows her from room to room, lies

next to her on the davenport while she's reading, sleeps with his head on her pillow, cries when she exits the room. This is what it is to be loved, to be needed, to be accepted as she is.

On Monday morning, her across-the-hall neighbor, Vilma, comes over and offers to walk Pip while she is at work. When she gets home that night, she finds two plates covered in waxed paper in front of her apartment door. Under one of the plates is a note: *I am a phone call away.* And then a number. It is from her neighbor, the bachelor baker, the one who plays Puccini over and over again. She knows that Martin has asked the man to keep an eye on her, but she still appreciates the kindness. She pulls out two chairs at the dining room table. Pip jumps onto one and she sits on the other. She eats the chocolate cake with her fingers and lets Pip eat the steak and baked potato from the plate.

On the Friday before Christmas Eve, Clementine gathers her purse and slips on her coat. It's already half past five, and she needs to get out the door and to the market before it closes. Martin isn't waiting in her outer office, so she asks her secretary to call up to the workshop.

"There's no answer, Miss Barman."

"Please keep trying," Clementine says. "If he answers, tell him I'm going to the market and will meet him back here by the main entrance as soon as I'm done."

Angela is behind the perfume counter, giftwrapping a purchase for a customer. She looks up and sees Clementine. Mouths, *wait!* Clementine waves, but keeps walking. On Riverside, she looks into the festively festooned window, and there is Martin fixing the arm of a tin soldier. She knocks, says *market* through the glass. Martin says, *wait*—but she doesn't. She walks down the street, looks up at the garlands of greenery strung across the avenue, the silver stars and bells. "Merry Christmas" is spelled out in lights; on the corner a Salvation Army Santa collects cast-off change.

She turns onto Post and is pulled sideways by someone in the crowd, pushed into the alley. The man from the warehouse. She screams, but it's lost in a cacophony of after-work sounds. He puts his hand over her mouth.

"Don't scream, baby. I just wanna be close to you. I've seen the way you look at me. I know you want it." Her struggle is making him hard. "Feel that?" he whispers into her ear. "That's what you do to me."

He puts his mouth on her neck, pushes his fingers into her, pushes her into the wall. He takes his hand off her mouth to undo his belt, unzip his pants. She screams again, and his hand comes down hard across her face. "I told you to keep your mouth shut, bitch." He tears at her panties and there is a crack, a shattering. Clementine opens her eyes and sees

Angela; she is holding a dust-covered high heel. A pile of painted plaster lays at their feet.

"Come here, love," says Angela. She takes Clementine in her arms, holds her until her sobs go silent. Finally, Clementine pulls back and asks, "How?"

"I hit him," Angela says, touching the plaster spot at the nape of Clementine's neck. "Here."

"But how did you know?"

"Because, darling, he was one of us."

Interlude: Clementine

Wondering how this story ends? Who gets the girl? Why, the one she was made for, of course.

However, there was no happy ending for this custom-made romance. Why, you ask? Because, one Sunday afternoon upon their return to the apartment—after their drive along the Sunset Highway—Martin climbed up on a chair to change an overhead light bulb, and, having had one too many martinis, fell and hit his head on the bedpost. When Clementine heard the clatter, she followed Pip's incessant barking to the back bedroom, but, alas, it was too late. All that remained of her beloved husband was a pile of plaster and his perfectly intact hand holding the spent light bulb.

Apartment D: The Bear
(1938)

Vilma tells her husband, Emil, that she doesn't want to go to the Junior League meeting, doesn't want to be away from their daughter, but he insists. She argues that Clara has never been left with a babysitter, in spite of the fact that she is almost six years old. Until now, there has never been a need for one. Emil does enough leaving for the both of them. Vilma sees no point in doing any leaving of her own.

"You need to get out and be seen," Emil says. "It looks good for business." He fixes his gaze on her. "It looks good for us."

It is past noon and Vilma is late for the meeting. She checks in with the nurse on duty at the playground inside the Crescent Department Store—the only option she has, since she has no real friends here. Not since Clementine, her across-the-hall neighbor, moved to Hollywood in the wake of her husband's death. Men, Vilma often thinks, are always disappearing. And if she is truly honest with herself, disappointing. She kisses Clara on the forehead.

"I'll be back before you miss me," she says.

Vilma walks as fast as she can to the towering, brick-faced Davenport Hotel. She is dizzy from not eating breakfast, dizzy from the early wave of spring heat.

"Circus Room," she tells the elevator operator.

When she enters the seventh-floor room, the dishes from the first course are being cleared: half-drunk glasses of pineapple juice and uneaten lettuce leaves wilting on salad plates. She takes the last seat at the table directly in front of the window. Perspiration instantly gathers in the dip of her throat, under her arms. A waitress sets a plate in front of her. On it is a thick slice of smoked tongue and a mound of potato salad. The animal smell of it almost knocks Vilma off her chair. She pales.

Is something wrong, dear? asks an egret of a woman, all neck and nose, at the head of the table. Her tone is condescending, her look pointed.

"Nothing at all," Vilma says, as she forces a smile. She spears a mayonnaised chunk of potato and puts it in her mouth. The awkwardness of the moment floats in the torpid air. Vilma waits for the woman to introduce herself, to introduce Vilma to the others at the table, but the woman does not. Instead, she acts as if Vilma isn't there, and the other women take the cue to ignore her as well.

Vilma reaches for a roll and breaks it into pieces while she listens to fragments of vapid conversations blooming around her: diamonds from Dodson's, a Christmas cruise to Honolulu, shoes from Schulein's, little Tommy's broken arm. Spots start to dance before her eyes, she feels faint—the lingering ghosts of another sleepless night. Despite the withering heat, she asks a passing waitress for a cup of coffee. She needs something to bolster her, to keep her going through the meeting. She stirs her coffee and looks around the room that the bird woman—who she learns is Mrs. Gumperfort, the chapter president—says was created as an homage to Harper Joy, a one-time circus clown and friend of Mr. Davenport. Vilma glances at the globes of colored lights in balloon bunches fighting to cast a glow over the table in the too-bright room, studies the mural with its parade of calliopes, camels, and clowns. Fixes her gaze on the bear that winks iridescent in the afternoon sunlight, moves in the waves of heat.

She slices the slab of tongue and hides the pieces under the lettuce garnish, so it looks as if she has eaten. The nauseating smell hits her anew. It makes her think of the day her mother boiled tongue for her grandmother. How it filled the house with an odor so awful, Vilma's father said, "Let's make a run for it, children." Then, laughing, he'd herded Vilma and her brother and sister into the barn and fed them chocolate bars and milk from their cow. Shortly after that day, her mother died while giving birth, leaving Vilma's father to raise four children on his own. What would her mother think of her daughter's escape from their small, North Dakota town? If

Vilma had stayed, she would be living a carefully prescribed life: she'd have a husband who worked the land and smelled of sweat and spring wheat, and four children, maybe five. She'd spend her days in the kitchen, her nights darning and mending, and her Sundays in church. Instead, she'd gotten on a train with her best friend, Anka, the day after they'd graduated from high school.

"Two tickets to Seattle," Anka said to the clerk. When the train pulled into Spokane's Great Northern Depot, she turned to Vilma and said, "Let's get off here."

"But we're still hours from Seattle," Vilma said, terrified.

"I dare you," Anka said. What could Vilma do after that? She got off the train.

In the beginning, she and Anka shared a room at the YWCA in the Rookery Building at Howard and Riverside. Anka went to work selling movie tickets at the newly opened Fox Theater. Vilma found a job in Intimate Fashions at the Crescent, where she sold brassieres and girdles to the ladies of the Lilac City. Once a week, she modeled dresses in the Tea Room's fashion shows. Anka left Spokane after seven months and returned to Vesta; Vilma remained. Emil came into her department one day and bought slips for the models at his furrier studio. He handed her his charge plate and asked her to dinner. In the middle of their first date, he invited her to model for him. She quit her job the next day.

Five months later they were married, seven months after that their daughter, Clara, was born. Would her mother be happy for her?

"Yes," she hears a voice say. "Very."

Was she speaking out loud? Embarrassed, she looks around to match the man's voice, low and dulcet, to a face—but she sees there are no men in the room. Even if she were talking to herself, no one here would be listening.

"Not true," says the same voice. "I am."

As soon as the dessert plates disappear, she gets up to go. No one looks in her direction, no one says goodbye. If no one acknowledges your presence, do you even exist? she wonders.

As Vilma exits the elevator, she sees a dark shadow pass behind a column in the lobby. She gasps and takes a step back.

"Are you okay, miss?" the elevator operator asks.

"Fine," she says distractedly. But is she?

Vilma stops in front of the Crescent and lights a cigarette before collecting Clara. Anka always said the building reminded her of a seven-layer ice box cake, and always made her hungry. The memory makes Vilma's empty stomach growl. She misses her silly, capricious friend and wonders if Anka misses her. She crushes her barely smoked cigarette into the sidewalk with the toe of her pump and goes inside to collect her daughter.

As they walk up Post to the Davenport Garage, Clara chatters about her two hours spent going up and down the slide and around and around on the merry-go-round. When they are backing out of their parking space, Clara says, "Mommy, I see a bear."

Vilma rolls down the window and lights another cigarette.

"Of course, you do, darling." Clara gets up on her knees and looks over the back seat. Waves as Vilma pulls out of the garage.

"Who are you waving to?" Vilma asks.

"The bear," Clara says. "He waved, so I waved back."

When Vilma and Clara arrive home, Emil is sitting on the davenport, flipping through a magazine.

"I stopped at Graham's," he says instead of *hello*, and motions toward the coffee table. Vilma looks down to a trio of her favorite magazines: *Vogue*, *Vanity Fair*, *The New Yorker*.

"What about me, Daddy?" says Clara.

He hands her a package wrapped in brown paper and tied with white string. Inside is a book of Norwegian fairy tales, on the cover an illustration of a bear with a girl riding on its back.

"I thought you and Mommy could read it while I'm gone," he says.

"I saw a bear—" Clara starts.

Vilma interrupts her. "Gone? Emil, what do you mean 'gone'?" Clara gives her mother a saucer-eyed look, and points to the bear on the cover. Vilma shakes her head, touches her index finger to her lips.

"Seattle, darling," he says.

"But you're leaving for Paris week after next."

"It's business, Vilma. I have to make money to keep you in frocks and baubles. If you don't fuss, maybe you'll get the fur coat you've been asking for."

"But I'd rather have you here," she says.

"Please don't start," says Emil.

The next afternoon Vilma packs Clara into the car, and drives downtown to the sky-scraping Paulsen Building for her standing appointment with Dr. Finklestein. She subsists on a diet of cigarettes, black coffee, and laxatives. Tries every new fad diet that comes out of Hollywood: the Hay (do not combine protein and starch), the Hollywood (grapefruit juice chasers after every meal), the one touted by Greta Garbo (heavy on Brewer's yeast, wheat germ, and molasses). The pills the doctor gives her help kill her appetite, keep her moving forward, keep her starlet thin.

After Vilma fills her prescription in the lobby's drugstore, she and Clara walk down Riverside to Modern Maid Ice Cream, and slide into a metal-edged, white vinyl booth.

"Chocolate ice cream and a cup of coffee," Vilma says to the waitress. "You have to get ice cream, too, Mommy," Clara says.

"Mommy has to watch her figure," Vilma says as she lights a cigarette. "For Daddy." If she gains a pound he notices. Comments. "You are a model," he reminds.

"Was, Emil, I was a model. Now I am a mother."

"Never lose your figure," he says. "Your looks are everything."

She resents the way he treats her, speaks to her. But after her uncertain beginning in Spokane, alone and broke in a city where she knew no one, being Emil's wife makes her feel secure, safe. "We taste with our eyes first," he says, quoting or misquoting a long forgotten lover of food, as his eyes travel over her body. She stays as perfect as she can for him. This husband of hers with his Vitalis-slick hair, his Errol Flynn mustache, his rakish smile. He is everything a woman could want. Almost.

Emil travels the world for business: Hawaii, Alaska, Chicago, New York, London, Argentina. "Our lovely expensive life," he says, as he casts his eyes over the furniture in their South Hill apartment: chromed, glassed, sharp-edged. Modern. "And my lovely, expensive wife," he also says, as he looks her over and walks out the door again and again and again.

Even when Emil is in Spokane, he's rarely at the apartment. Vilma finds a matchbook from a pool hall, after he told her he was at the studio until 2:00 a.m. working on a custom fur for Miss Spokane. Weeks later, she finds another from a tavern on Trent. Weeks after that, a receipt for a motor lodge on the Sunset Highway.

"I took one of our suppliers to a roadhouse," he says. "We got cross-eyed drunk and needed a place to sleep it off."

She tries to imagine her elegant husband in an inelegant roadhouse, a motor inn. She tries to imagine him dead drunk. Somehow she just can't see it.

Sometimes Emil returns from his weekends away with a black eye, bruises in the shape of a hand on his upper arms, bite marks on his thighs. After her first year of marriage, she stopped asking questions. She got tired of the excuses, tired of the screaming, tired of being tired.

"Shrew," he would accuse. She learned to ignore, she learned to pretend.

"Ma'am?" the waitress says, as she sets Vilma's coffee in front of her. Makes a point of leaving two spoons in front of the parfait cup, thinking they will share. This innocent Modern Maid in her white dress—collared, cuffed, starched—and her paper hat worn like a tiara has no idea what a bite of anything unplanned can do to upend Vilma's day.

Clara runs her finger over the chocolate soft-serve melting over the edge of the cup and licks it. Vilma takes a sip of her coffee. It scalds her tongue.

"Mommy, it's the bear. I see the bear," Clara says.

Vilma encourages Clara's imagination, her tall tales. Never ignores her.

"Do you see him, Mommy? Do you?" Vilma follows the line of her daughter's pointed finger across the street.

"I'm sure—" she starts. And that's when she spots the bear, peeking around the corner of the Mohawk Building looking right at her.

Vilma stands in the dark bedroom and looks out over the apartment's garage at the rooflines that run up Adams. At the end of the line, the moon is competing with the stars for attention. Behind her, Clara is asleep on Emil's side of the bed, the side that is empty more often than it is occupied. Vilma presses her forehead to the glass and closes her eyes. Thinks, *Emil.* There is a knock on the window. She opens her eyes to a bear, his paws and face pressed to the glass.

Before Vilma can react, Clara is out of bed and moving toward the window. She stands next to Vilma and puts her face on the glass, her hands. The bear lowers his head until they are nose to nose. He motions for Clara to open the window. She is too small to push it up on her own, so Vilma does it for her.

She pulls Clara aside as the bear somersaults into the room and lands with a thud on the hardwood floor.

"You found us," Clara says.

"I did," the bear says as he rights himself. Clara sits next to him, can't take her eyes off of him.

"What's your name?" Clara asks.

"Boris," he answers.

Vilma sits on the edge of the bed. She feels dizzy and anxious, as if she's taken too many diet pills.

"Where did you come from?" Vilma asks.

"The Circus Room," he says. "I was there and now I am here."

"I don't understand," Vilma says.

"It's okay," he says. "Neither do I. Not really."

"How did you find me? Us?" asks Vilma.

"I followed the scent of your sadness," he says.

"What does sadness smell like?" Clara asks.

"Burnt sugar," he says. Vilma lifts her arm to her nose, breathes deeply. Searches for the scent he smelled on her skin.

Vilma and Clara walk Boris down the hall, into the living room. He settles onto the rug between the fireplace and the davenport.

"Why me?" Vilma asks.

"You seemed so far away, so sad. It drew me to you, your sadness," he says. "Also, most people don't even notice me.

They see the tigers and lions; the rhinos and hippos; the clowns and rajas. But me? No one pays attention to a brown bear. But you did. You saw me. Being seen is its own kind of magic," he says. She nods. Understands.

"Was it you talking to me in the Circus Room?" Vilma asks.

"Yes," he says.

"And was that you by the garage last night?"

He smiles. "Yes."

"I thought it was a man in a fur coat," Vilma says.

"In May?" Boris says. Their laughter is a chorus.

Boris tells Vilma and Clara that he and his parents were in the circus. His father danced, his mother walked on her front paws. It was a joyless existence but the three of them were together. A family. When the Depression ravaged the country, people didn't have money to go to the circus, which meant that there wasn't money to take care of the animals. His mother died first. Starvation. Then his father. Shot when he mauled a clown. "Hunger and grief," says Boris, "are a combustible combination." Then: "I was left alone without anyone to care for me. Mr. Joy, one of the clowns, took pity on me. He fed me, brushed me, loved me. But the circus had no use for a cub who couldn't do tricks. 'A burden,' the trainer said. 'A mouth to feed.' I was shot in my cage as I slept. It was August. Mr. Joy cried when he heard the news. It was his warm-heartedness that kept my spirit alive."

Clara holds his paw as he tells his story. Vilma strokes his fur and watches as it changes color: chocolate brown to brown shot with gold and turquoise. She is ashamed that she thought wearing fur was glamorous. "Forgive me," she says. They talk until the sky is melted strawberry ice cream spreading over the city. Clara snuggles into Boris's fur and falls asleep. Vilma pulls the coverlet off the back of the davenport and lies down next to them. Covers herself and Clara, then sinks into a deep, silent sleep.

Over the course of a week, Vilma, Clara, and Boris fall into a routine. Vilma wakes at seven and makes pancakes with huckleberry jam. Pours coffee for herself, milk for Boris and Clara. Clara and Boris make the beds, while Vilma washes the dishes. Then Boris follows Vilma from room to room. Asks her questions. Wants to hear her stories. She tells him everything that she cannot tell anyone else. An unburdening, she thinks. On the day Emil is set to return, Boris kisses Clara and Vilma on the forehead and crawls out the window onto the fire escape.

"Where will you go?" Vilma asks.

"I'll hide, wait."

"But Boris," she says.

"Don't worry," he says. "I'll be back in a week."

Emil arrives with a pyramid of boxes from Frederick &

Nelson. For Vilma, a blue-and-white, short-sleeved, full-skirted Elizabeth Hawes dress. For Clara, a candy-colored romper and a tin of Frango mints. He tells Vilma to clear her schedule for the week.

"We, darling, are going to host an off-to-Paris party." He raises his hands in the air as if reading a motion picture star's name on a marquee. "Woodland-themed. Costumes a must." He pauses and looks at her. "A beautiful party, for beautiful people."

"But Emil," she says, "it will be your last night in Spokane . . . for weeks."

"What better reason to celebrate?" he says. Touches his index finger to the tip of her nose.

On the night of the party, the guests arrive in various configurations: twos, threes, fives. A coterie of pretty girls and equally pretty boys. Emil's models and their acolytes—ethereal, vapid, vain. A heady, impossible-to-resist combination. *The Not-So-Innocents*, Emil calls them.

An hour into the party, the door swings open, and a solitary guest stands in the doorway. His hair is blonde, his eyes blue, his skin spun sugar. He is wearing a wisp of an evergreen satin costume with moss-green tights, a cap, and booties made of fur. Vilma watches as Emil moves toward the door, pulls him close, kisses him on each cheek, whispers something in his ear. The gesture is intimate, familiar.

Emil walks the man over to Vilma. "My wife," he says.

"Hello, wife," the man says, taking her hand and kissing it. "I am Peter," he says. "Prince of the Forest," he adds.

There are bottles of champagne, plates of petits fours, caviar, cocaine. Boys kissing boys and girls kissing boys. The models pretend Vilma is adored, but she isn't. She is tolerated by all, scoffed at by some. She is a wife, a mother. It is not an equation they care to understand or accept.

It is after two when Emil closes the door behind the last of the guests. He crosses the room and kisses Vilma. It is fervent, all tongue. He tastes like gin and cigarettes. "Take off your dress," he says. He unbuttons his trousers, bends her over the back of the couch, slips her panties to the side, and enters her from behind. He holds her hips, does not touch her breasts. Pulls her hair. Calls her *bitch*, calls her *whore*.

"Emil, stop," she says. But he's not listening. Sex with him is always rough, happens only when he is drunk. Is always only, as he says, *fucking*. She was eighteen when she met him. She didn't know all men weren't like this.

Fifteen minutes after Emil leaves the next morning, Vilma hears rapping on the bedroom window.

"It's Boris," Clara hollers. She leaves her fork standing

in a triangle of pancakes. "Hurry, Mommy," she calls as she bolts down the hall. Vilma opens the window and Boris somersaults in. A repeat of his first entrance into their lives. Clara is tripping over her words as she pulls Boris back to the table. Vilma makes him a triple stack, swimming in maple syrup, pours him a glass of milk. She appreciates his boundless appetite.

"You eat like a bear," her father often said to her, and laughed as he ruffled her hair, and served her a second helping of lefse or lutefisk. Vilma pats them both on the head. Leaves them—Clara and her bear brother—to talk and catch up.

Vilma makes a cherry pie for dinner. She and Clara and Boris sit on a blanket on the living room floor and eat it straight from the pie pan.

"A family picnic," Boris says.

"To family," Vilma says. They clang their forks together in a jammy toast.

The day of the Lilac Parade arrives. Boris and Clara have been talking about it all week. Vilma and Clara bundle Boris into the car. It is their first outing together. Vilma and Clara wear matching lilac dresses. Clara ties a ribbon around Boris's neck—also lilac. Vilma turns the radio to their favorite station and drives down Lincoln toward the parade route.

"Get up close," Boris says. "I'll watch from the car."

Vilma parks backwards, so Boris can stretch his arms across

the seat, press his nose to the rearview window, see what she and Clara see.

"If someone walks by," Vilma tells him, "play dead." He rolls his eyes back and lets his tongue loll sideways.

"Not quite like that, Boris," she says laughing.

Vilma and Clara choose a spot on the edge of the sidewalk: watch the solitary float go by, the seven decorated cars. Men walk the edge of the parade route handing out lilac shoots. The street is a happy profusion of purple and white.

After the parade, Vilma and Clara walk toward the car, but don't see Boris.

"Mommy, he's gone," says Clara. Her eyes crowd with tears. "How can we live without him?" she asks.

"I don't know," says Vilma. She cannot give Clara a grown-up answer because she doesn't have one. Just then they see his head pop up out of the back seat. Vilma opens the car door.

"Boris!" she says. "We were so scared you'd gone."

"Gone? Where would I go?" he says. "A policeman passed the car, and I had to pretend to be a fur blanket. Then I fell asleep. Pretending is exhausting," he says. Vilma rubs his ear. "I know," she says. "I know." She leans in and kisses him on the nose.

One Tuesday afternoon, Vilma and Clara sneak Boris out of

the apartment and into the back seat of the car.

"Where are we going?" Boris asks.

"You'll see," Vilma says.

She drives through their neighborhood, past houses that Boris calls *fancy*.

"Daddy says we live here because we are movers and shakers," says Clara.

"What's a *mover shaker*?" asks Boris.

"Someone who does this," Clara says and shimmies her shoulders.

The two shimmy and laugh block after block, but when they drive through the entrance of Manito Park, Boris holds his paws over his ears. Shakes his head back and forth.

"The sound," Boris says.

"What sound?" Vilma asks.

"Death," he says.

"Oh, Boris," she says. Then she remembers. "There was a zoo here once, but at the start of the Depression, it closed," says Vilma. "Some of the animals were sent to other zoos, some were released into the wild, and some," she pauses, "were shot." Clara gasps. Boris nods. As if their end was an expectation, not an exception.

"Cruel," Boris says.

"Cruel," Clara echoes.

Once a week, Vilma goes to the fishmonger to buy slabs of

salmon—three, sometimes five. These Boris eats raw right out of the icebox. She buys baskets of berries from the fruit vendor. These she bakes into pies. She also buys jars of honey, bottles of Coca-Cola, stacks of Hershey bars. However, there is nothing Boris loves more than hamburgers. Every Friday night Vilma and Clara sneak Boris down the fire escape after sunset. He climbs into the back seat of the car, and they cover him with a blanket for their drive to Top Hat Drive-In. They order cheeseburgers, French fries, and milkshakes—always chocolate. When they arrive at their spot by the river, Boris throws off his blanket and Clara pulls their food from the bag. For the next hour, they eat, laugh, and sing along to Friday-night radio songs.

Every afternoon at three, Vilma, Clara, and Boris sit down for a long coffee break. Vilma splashes coffee into the bottom of two tiny teacups. For Boris and Clara, she adds milk and sugar until the coffee is white and tastes like candy; she pours a cup for herself and drops in two cubes of sugar. The three of them eat cookies—molasses, sugar, icebox—and make plans for how they will carry out this daily ritual when Emil returns. After coffee, Vilma reads from Clara's book of fairy tales; Clara and Boris love the stories about bears most of all.

Boris sleeps next to Clara's bed, her hand is always resting on his head as she falls asleep. He tells her tales of his life in the circus. Makes up stories of what his life might have been like in the forest—he adds princes and princesses, sometimes a witch.

On nights that Boris doesn't get enough to eat, he opens the window and crawls down the fire escape. His destination is always the same: the garbage cans. Vilma puts on her robe and slippers, coaxes him back into the house, apologizes, and makes him a midnight snack.

The summer days loop into each other—become weeks, months. Vilma gains seven pounds, sleeps eight hours a night, laughs until she can't breathe, is happy as soon as she opens her eyes.

One Thursday, Vilma packs a picnic lunch: sweet onion and butter sandwiches, bread-and-butter pickles, cherry tarts. She drives from Spokane to Priest River, while Clara and Boris make up stories in the back seat. When they arrive in the North Idaho town, Vilma sees a sign singing from a rooftop: "Hotel Charbonneau." She follows it and finds a tiny triangle of a gas station on the corner. A man with a name tag that reads CHARLIE fills up the tank. Vilma gets out to buy three bottles of Coke from the vending machine and asks the man about a picnic spot. He tells her to take the bridge across the river. "Turn right at the end. Drive until you see a little red cabin. Buddy Moore owns it. Nice fella. He won't mind if you spend the day there." She thanks him and hands him a dollar for gas.

Vilma crosses the bridge and drives down the river-fronting dirt road until she finds the cabin. It is tucked between an inlet on one side and a forest on the other. A perfect place to spend the day. If anyone pulls into the makeshift driveway, Boris can dart into the stand of trees near the creek or into the woods.

After the tarts have been eaten, the last sips of Coke drunk, Vilma lies back on the blanket and lets the sun hit her face. Listens to the river waves lapping the shore. Listens to Clara and Boris playing hide-and-seek between the pine trees. Soon summer will come to an end. Soon Emil will return from Paris. Soon Clara will start first grade. But right now, time is standing still.

A week after their return from Idaho, Vilma walks in the door from her trip to Krohl's Market. She pulls off her gloves, reaches up to unfasten her clip-on earrings, and finds that one is missing.

"My earring," she says to Clara and Boris. "It must have slipped off when I called you from the pay phone downtown. I wore them to Priest River. They remind me of our day together."

"You start dinner," Boris says. "And I will go and look

for it."

"Boris, no," says Vilma. "Someone might see you."

"Don't worry, I'll be back before you can say—"

"Jack Robinson," he and Clara say in unison.

Vilma and Clara watch as he crawls out the back window and down the fire escape. When he reaches the sidewalk, he looks up and waves before lumbering down Adams. Forty-five minutes later, the front door opens.

"Surprise!" It's Emil. His appearance is abrupt, unexpected. Vilma looks at Clara, Clara looks at Vilma. "No," Clara mouths. Vilma pales with disappointment. Boris does not return. He is not in the garage. Is not on the fire escape. Is not napping in the back corner of the laundry room.

The next morning over coffee, Emil looks over the top of the paper at Vilma. Tells her a bear was seen downtown. Laughs at the idea of it peeking into the windows of the Crescent, having tea at the Davenport.

Vilma stays in bed for a week. Does not eat. Loses the seven pounds she gained. Returns to Dr. Finkelstein for pills. Snaps at Clara when she asks for ice cream.

The following Friday, Emil promises to be home for dinner at six—it is now eleven. Vilma tries calling the studio, but Emil does not answer. Should she call the police? The hospital?

Instead, she wakes Clara, carries her to the car, drives downtown. She parks in front of the studio and leaves her sleeping on the front seat. It is reckless, but she is desperate and fraught with worry. She imagines the worst, as is her way. Vilma lets herself into the building—walks past the showroom, the offices. She sees a light on in the studio and hears a voice.

"Emil?" she says, as she pushes the door open and starts to walk in. There is her husband leaning against the cutting table. His eyes closed, his head back, a man in front of him on his knees, Emil's hands cupping the man's head. She turns and trips over an unopened box. She hears Emil call her name as she runs down the hall. It bounces and echoes off the silent walls.

When Vilma arrives back at the apartment, she is shaking. The bruise on her shin blooming blue.

At midnight, Emil walks in the door and finds Vilma staring out the balcony window into the dark. He stands next to her, says her name. Apologizes for not coming home for dinner, but does not make an excuse for what she saw. She turns, her eyeshadow smeared, her face mascara-streaked.

"Why?" she asks.

"You know who I am, Vilma. You knew when you married me. You can't possibly be upset." He takes her face in his hands. "It doesn't mean I don't love you, darling. I just love you . . . differently."

She pulls away from him. "I hate you!" she screams. "I hate you! I hate you! I hate you!" Her voice gets higher and louder with each exclamation. She tears at his chest, at his hair. She wants to hurt him the way he's hurt her. The air around them is charged, electric.

"Vilma, stop!" he says. He holds her wrists. Waits for her to stop thrashing.

"I wish you were dead!" she screams. "Do you hear me? Dead!"

"Why, Mommy?" She turns and Clara is standing at the edge of the living room. Only then, embarrassed and defeated, does she stop.

"Shameful," Emil says under his breath. The victory, as always, is his.

A week later, Clementine calls. "I'm in town and I want to see you. Put on your prettiest dress and meet me at the Tea Room tomorrow. Noon. And bring my little love, Clara."

"I don't think—" Vilma starts.

"No excuses," Clementine interrupts. "I've already reserved the table and ordered the cake."

"But my birthday isn't until next week," Vilma says.

"It's never too early to celebrate."

At eleven the next morning, Vilma dresses Clara and then stands in front of her closet deciding what to wear. Finally she pulls an unworn dress from its hanger, fastens the straps of her shoes, powders her nose, applies a coat of lipstick. For the first time in weeks, she feels—not exactly happy—but ready to go out and be around other people.

She drives downtown and parks in the Davenport Garage. Thinks of Boris and how Clara first spotted him here. Where did you go, Boris? she wonders. Why didn't you say goodbye?

There is a chill in the September air signaling the shift from summer to fall. Vilma and Clara walk down Post toward the Crescent. When they turn onto Riverside, they see Clementine walking toward them.

Hollywood has made her even more glamorous. She looks like a movie star in a purple, gored skirt embroidered with dancing, blue ponies, and a pink jacket with trapeze artist buttons cast in metal climbing up the front. An ensemble from Schiaparelli's *Circus Collection* that Vilma saw on the pages of *Vogue*.

"My girls," Clementine says.

They take the express elevator to the Tea Room, where the hostess seats them behind a bank of potted palms that, in this wide open room, affords a small wall of privacy.

"How are you, Vilma?" Clementine asks.

I caught my husband cheating on me . . . with a man, she wants to say, but doesn't. *My life is a lie. My best friend is a bear.*

"Nothing ever really changes," she says. A truth and an untruth, so not exactly a lie, she reasons.

Models wearing dresses from the fall collection move through the room. Every few minutes, a different woman stops at their table, announces the name of the designer she is wearing, the department where it can be purchased, the price. Vilma is one bite into her shrimp salad when she hears a voice stereoing from the other side of the potted palm. Vilma recognizes the woman's voice as the ringleader of the Junior League circus: Mrs. Gumperfort.

"Did I tell you, Ethel," Mrs. Gumperfort continues, "Melvin bought me a mink for our twenty-fifth wedding anniversary?"

"A mink?" Ethel says, her voice tinged green.

"Yes, from the fairy with the shop on Madison," Mrs. Gumperfort says. "The one who married his model." The women erupt in a fit of wicked laughter.

Vilma gasps. The comment slices, mortifies. Is it that obvious?

"Jealous," Clementine says.

Vilma opens her mouth to explain, deflect, but nothing comes out. She cannot speak. Clementine takes her hand under the table, says, "We all have our secrets, Vilma."

The day of Vilma's twenty-fifth birthday arrives. Clementine insists she go out with Emil to celebrate, tells her she will watch Clara.

"You can't hide in your apartment forever," she says.

Vilma puts on her new black Balenciaga dress—from Emil, from Paris. Dabs Chanel No. 5 behind her ears, the dip of her throat, the insides of her wrists—also from Emil, also from Paris. He takes her to dinner at Louis Crillo's. They order steak, spaghetti, a bottle of red wine. She is tired of being angry, tired of being sad, tired of pretending she and Emil are anything other than what they are—a couple with an arrangement. Emil reaches across the table and strokes her hand.

"I have a surprise for you when we get home," he says.

"I love surprises," she says.

"I know, sweetheart. I know," he says.

Emil parks the car in the garage behind the apartment. Vilma looks to the left, the right.

"Boris?" she whispers.

"Vilma?" Emil asks.

"Nothing," she answers.

Inside, Emil pulls the cage door of the elevator closed, turns the lever to take them to the third floor. She can smell Boris's earthy smell—wet leaves and sunshine.

"Do you smell that?" she asks Emil.

"Smell what?" he says.

Emil unlocks the door, flips on the light, leads her to the davenport, kisses her on the cheek.

"Close your eyes," he says.

He sets a box on her lap. She opens her eyes, pulls the ribboned bow, lifts the lid, casts aside the layers of tissue paper. Notices the label first: "B. Furriers, Spokane, Washington."

"I designed it for you, darling," he says.

She pulls the coat from the box. It is puff-sleeved and pleated, nipped in at the waist. She strokes the brown fur and watches as it throws off sparks of gold and turquoise. The realization rends.

"Remember the headline?" Emil says. "The bear downtown?"

She can feel bile rising, she swallows her scream. Brings the coat to her face and vomits into the fur of her friend.

"You've ruined it," Emil says. "You've destroyed your coat."

"And you," she says with tears rivering down her face, "have destroyed me."

Interlude: Vilma

A chaplet of weeks after what Emil calls "the fur incident"—and Vilma considers the worst night of her life—she finds a crumpled cocktail napkin from the Silver Grill at the Spokane Hotel in the pocket of Emil's coat. She expects to find a name, a phone number—instead there is a single line written in Emil's handwriting: "I am a constellation of scars." Below it is a sketch of the Eiffel Tower.

She smooths the napkin and tucks it into the back of her panty drawer. Saves it as a reminder that the heartbreak of this marriage does not belong to her alone.

Apartment E: The Dandelion (1958)

At the exact moment Edwina Hemplemeyer's husband, Harold, was hit by a taxi, she was eating a Swanson's TV dinner for lunch and watching her favorite soap opera, *Search for Tomorrow.*

At the exact moment Harold stepped in front of the taxi, he was eating one of the thirteen éclairs he'd bought for his wife, Edwina. The signal flashed WALK. He closed his eyes, lifted his face to the sun, stepped off the curb, and smacked into a taxi making a right-hand turn. There were screams and the screech of brakes. Harold heard nothing but his own sigh of pleasure. His last words, *Edwina.* Then, *éclair.*

At the exact moment Harold died, the balcony door of Harold's and Edwina's apartment gusted open, and the fried chicken leg Edwina was gnawing on flew out of her hand. Lucy, their dachshund, who looked alarmingly like Edwina, raced toward it and swallowed it whole. "You stupid creature," Edwina screamed. The dog had deprived her of the pleasure of stripping the bone clean—sucking on it until it looked polished, prehistoric.

Early one Saturday morning, one month before Harold

died, two children arrived at Mt. Vernon Apartments. First a little boy, then a little girl. The boy had a round face, pale brown skin, and Elvis Presley hair. He wore a white T-shirt and dungarees, dark and cuffed deep. His name was Teddy. He had come with his grandpa, Mr. Aikura, to help rake the leaves and trim the bushes.

The girl, whose name was Darla, pulled up in an ocean-blue Ford Fairlane with her grandma, Vilma. Darla had almond eyes, olive skin, and two long black braids with bangs cut blunt across her forehead. Her father was a diplomat, her mother a model. Work sent them to Paris. Darla, it was decided, would stay with her grandma until the school year ended, until her parents got settled.

Edwina watched as the little girl crossed the lawn, watched as red mushrooms spotted with white popped up with every step she took. Edwina blinked, but the mushrooms remained. She felt blood moving to her temples, felt one of her spells coming on. She watched as the little girl walked up to the little boy, stuck out her hand, and introduced herself. Witch, thought Edwina. "Precocious," she said out loud. "How vile." Edwina hated children. Their unnecessary messes, their insufferable laughter.

"How old are you?" Teddy asked Darla.

"Eight," she said. "You?"

He straightened. "Ten and a half," he said with a smile. Darla looked up and saw Edwina's face pressed against the glass, her scowl visible from below. "Why is she staring at us?" Darla asked Teddy. "Maybe she's lonely," he said. "Maybe she needs a friend." He handed Darla half of his chocolate chip cookie. "Maybe," Darla said, taking a bite, "she's just mean."

One Tuesday afternoon, three weeks before Harold died, he brought Edwina a pink bakery box containing twelve éclairs. She took it and put it in the cupboard. When he suggested they share a sweet before dinner, she scolded him. Told him he was older now and needed to watch his blood pressure, his weight. This she said as she stared at the space between his concave chest and jutting hipbones. "You have a paunch," she declared, and shook her head in disgust. In the morning, the bakery box was empty, crumbs marched across the counter and spilled onto the floor. Harold had heard her purring in the kitchen as she ate one éclair after the other. He imagined her running her fork through the middle of the pastry—shredding it, as he had seen her do to an entire roast chicken—crowding bite after bite into her gaping, painted mouth. After that he bought thirteen éclairs and made sure to eat his before he got home.

The week before Harold died, Teddy arrived at Darla's

grandma's apartment with a clown tucked under his arm.

"What is that?" Darla asked when she saw the small, sad-faced hobo.

"Willie," he said. "My grandpa bought him for me."

"He's scary," Darla said. Teddy laughed and chased her around the yard with the clown for the rest of the afternoon. From behind the curtain Edwina watched the children play. The clown had the same beaten-down look as her husband. His sad face infuriated her. Stupid clown, she thought. She saw the doll look up at her from where Darla had propped him against the tree. He shook his head, raised his index finger, and wagged it at her. She let the curtain fall and called her husband in a panic.

"It sounds like you are having one of your spells," Harold said. "Take a pill and lie down."

"I know what I saw," she said, her voice thin and frantic.

"Yes, dear," he said.

"You stupid, stupid man," she screeched, before slamming the receiver into its cradle.

She banged on the window and screamed "Shut up!" at the children. She could not stand another second of their happiness. Teddy and Darla looked up and waved.

On the day Harold died, Edwina said, "You're not dying today," when Harold reminded her of his late morning doctor's appointment. Dr. Pinkerling echoed her words, and told Harold to drink milk for his ulcer and then sent him off with a stronger prescription for his nerve pills. These Harold gave to Edwina for her daily spells—caused, she told him, by his stupidity. His inability to tackle the smallest household task. He loved his wife, even if he wasn't good enough for her, man enough for her. He knew Edwina was right, she was always right. However, on this particular Tuesday, she was wrong.

On the day Harold died, Edwina opened the door to two policemen, one young and one old, there to deliver the news of Harold's accident. His death. Her first thought: widow. Her second: insurance. She made a great show of emotion in front of the policemen: put the back of her hand to her forehead, asked to be carried to the couch. The men looked at her and then at each other. They took her by the elbows and guided her to the nearest chair, which happened to be Harold's.

"I need cake," she said to the younger of the two. "Nerves," she said. As he walked toward the kitchen, she called out, "Don't forget the milk."

When they left, she raced down the hall to Harold's room, and riffled through the filing cabinet until she found his life insurance policy. When she saw the "payable on death" amount, she threw her plump arms into the air. "Thank you, Jesus!" she cried out and fell onto her dimpled knees.

Harold was a hypochondriac. He'd learned early in life that when he was sick, he got his mother's attention, even if fleetingly. He'd learned later in life that when he was sick he got his wife's attention, even if fleetingly. Harold suffered from headaches, stomachaches, backaches—if there was an ache Harold had it.

Harold sold life insurance policies. He was a frugal man, but when it came to insurance his motto was, "Less is never more." Harold believed in insurance the way other men believed in sex or God.

Harold wore shades of brown from head to toe: tan, taupe, khaki, beige—sometimes chocolate, sometimes caramel. His hair was brown, his eyes were brown, his skin was not. He had the sad eyes of a pig being sent to slaughter. He was not handsome, nor was he ugly. He was an average, nondescript man, a slump-shouldered letter S. Harold was forty-seven years old.

"Younger," he teased Edwina.

Edwina was a bold letter B. She wore Christmas-colored dresses, always ruby or emerald, in the fit-and-flare cut. The bodice showcased the stack of her breasts, the skirt hid the swell of her belly. Her shoes, peep-toed and ankle-strapped, matched her dresses. Her hair was coal black—clipped and straightened into a German helmet. She powdered her sallow, speckled skin white, colored her cheeks with circles of rouge. Made her mouth into an *O*, and traced the shape with cherry-red lipstick. Her most defining feature was her finch-beaked nose. Edwina Hemplemeyer was forty-nine years old but told everyone she was thirty-three.

Edwina was a gossip, a busybody, a snoop. When she wasn't yelling at Harold or watching television or the comings and goings of her neighbors from behind the curtain, she listened in on the party line. It was one of her favorite things to do. If she heard the phone ring, she raced to pick it up, even if it wasn't the special ring assigned to her line. She'd hold her breath and listen. If the conversation was particularly juicy, she'd forget herself and gasp or tsk.

One bright blue Saturday morning, three days before Harold died, he took Lucy for a walk. He did not return in the ten minutes Edwina had allowed. She was ready to be driven to the drugstore and did not like to be kept waiting. She peered over the balcony and saw Harold laughing with the gardener. The children were on their knees petting Lucy.

"Harold! It's time to go," she hollered.

Harold waved. "I'll be right up, dear," he hollered back.

"Now!" she screamed. She saw Harold's cheeks color tomato. He said something to the old man and the children.

It looked like *sorry*. Harold walked in the door holding a Tupperware container. "How dare you make me wait!" she said. Spit flew from her mouth and hit Harold in the eye.

"What is that?" she asked, her face lemon sour.

"Lunch," he said, "for us." He smiled, which angered her even more. "Mr. Aikura's wife made it. It's called ramen. We just have to heat it up and crack an egg on top." She took the green plastic bowl from his hands and marched into the kitchen, pulled off the lid, and turned the bowl upside down into the trash bin. "Edwina!" he said. "Why?" Disappointment colored his question.

"I don't eat strange food from strange people!" she shrieked, and threw the bowl into the sink.

"Strange? He's no stranger than you or me," he said.

"He is nothing like me," she said. "He looks nothing like me." Her voice was fingernails on a chalkboard.

"Have you forgotten, Edwina, who you are? Where you're from?" Harold questioned.

"Don't say it!" She lifted her fist. Shook it. "Don't you dare say it." Her voice punctuated the final word so it became a capital *I*, a capital *T*. She opened the cupboard and ripped open a package of Twinkies. She pushed one into her mouth and then another. She pulled at the elastic of her blouse that had inched up her belly, exposing a pale gray roll of fat. When she turned to Harold, she was shrink-wrapped by a plastic calm.

"Sit," she said. "If you're so hungry, I'll make you lunch."

She motioned toward the dining room table. Harold obeyed. She brought him a sandwich (white bread slathered with mayonnaise, a slice of American cheese, two rounds of bologna), a pickle; a glass of milk.

"Now that," she said, pointing to his plate, "is a normal lunch for a normal person. Eat!"

Most days, Harold woke up happy, and Edwina woke up mad. Harold sang while he made them coffee, sang while he added sugar and cream, sang while he showered. Edwina screamed at him to stop. "No one," she said, "wants to hear your ridiculous warble."

The only time that Edwina wasn't mad was for a single hour on Sunday nights. She would send Harold to his room with his turkey TV dinner (never fried chicken; those were hers and hers alone). She would turn on the television, wait for it to warm up, and switch the selector knob to Channel 2. When Ed Sullivan appeared, Edwina would let out a porcine squeal, and peel back the foil of her own TV dinner. First, she would scoop the buttered mashed potatoes into her mouth, then the mixed vegetables—rounds of green peas and cubes of carrots—then on to the chicken, which she ate from the smallest piece to the largest. When the chicken was gone, she lifted the tray to her face and licked each compartment clean. She repeated the ritual with her second TV dinner, which she ate more slowly than the first. By the time she licked the second tray clean, the sixty-minute program was ending. Her mood switched from not-mad to mad. Fast.

"Harold," she bellowed down the hall. Each week she made up a malady before he reached the living room. He took her aluminum trays to the kitchen and returned with a quarter of a coconut cream pie.

"Eat this, dear, it will make you feel better." She took it from him and waved him away.

Instead of "Thank you," she said, "Go back to your room and leave me alone." Once sated, she would burp three times, the second louder than the first, and the third, Harold's signal that he was allowed back into the living room because she was ready for a sleep. Allowed to sit in his chair by the window and read the paper. He'd look at Edwina asleep on the couch, snoring, then at Lucy asleep in his lap, also snoring. A perfect night, he'd think.

Ladies who knew Harold and Edwina from church, Harold's office, and Edwina's bridge club arrived with casseroles, cakes, and sympathy. Edwina put away her holiday-hued ensembles, dressed only in black, wore a lace scarf over her head. Made a show of being a widow. When she looked in the mirror, she saw an Italian movie star.

On the first day of May, Teddy and Darla picked a child-sized armful of lilacs and tied them with a white satin ribbon from Darla's grandma's sewing basket. They opened the door to the cage elevator, got in, and turned the lever to the right to take them to the second floor. They tiptoed to Edwina's apartment, laid the flowers in front of her door, and knocked. Hollered "Happy May Day!" then ran down the stairs to the landing. They waited, listened. Put their hands over their mouths to stifle their laughter. Edwina opened the door and quickly slammed it.

"She got them," they whispered excitedly.

"Think they'll make her happy?" asked Darla.

"Lilacs make everyone happy," said Teddy. They were still laughing when they got to their spot under the maple tree.

"Do you think she'll know they were from us?" said Darla.

"No," said Teddy. "We were too fast." He made a zigzag motion with his arm. "Like lightning."

"Oh no," Darla exclaimed. Dismay rained over her small face. "Look." She pointed to a patch of grass under Edwina's window. There lay the lilacs—the ribbon undone, the flowers scattered.

After Harold died, Edwina filled the freezer with Swanson's TV dinners—all fried chicken. Told the milkman to cancel the skim milk, the eggs; told him to bring whole milk only: plain and chocolate. She added strawberry ice cream to the order, an extra bottle of cream. Now that Harold was dead, she didn't have to worry about his weight, his growing belly.

After Harold died, Edwina bought a new wardrobe at the Crescent: Day, Evening, and Resort. She sold Harold's old car and bought a new one. It was pink, impractical, perfect. She booked a first-class cruise to Hawaii to ring in 1959 at the Royal Hawaiian in Honolulu. She told anyone who would listen about the possibility of a torrid love affair with a Hawaiian beach boy.

After Harold died, Edwina kept Lucy in the baby cage that was wired to the window in the smallest of the three bedrooms. Lucy, like the baby who had occupied the cage two decades before her, spent her time there in a state of perpetual lassitude. Lucy missed Harold and bemoaned this new version of her life. She cried from the time Edwina put her in the cage until she took her out eight hours later. Edwina told a woman from her church group that she couldn't stand Lucy's theatrics, her tears. One month to the day after Harold's death, Edwina marched Lucy up the stairs and handed her leash to the neighbor—the one everyone called the *bachelor baker*. She told him she had no use for Lucy, could not possibly be expected to deal with her whining or her constant need for attention. The man opened his door a little wider and welcomed the dog into his life.

One Wednesday afternoon, while playing bridge, Edwina turned to the woman on her right. She was feeling peckish. Mean.

"Sylvie, you've lost weight."

The woman nodded. Did not say that her husband had left her. That he was having an affair. That she had stopped eating.

"You look," Edwina continued, "like a lollipop."

"Excuse me?" Sylvie said.

"Your head," said Edwina, "is too big for your body." Edwina slid her hand down the front of her dress, her hills of flesh. "Men," she informed her, "like women with curves." She shoved a tuna finger sandwich into her mouth and turned to the woman on her left. She was new to the club—sophisticated, stylish, beautiful. Edwina hated her on sight.

"Liliana, is it?" she asked, and held out her mayonnaise-smeared fingers.

"Yes," the woman smiled and took Edwina's greasy fingers in her hand.

"You're so dark," Edwina said, eyeing her brown skin with disdain.

"My grandmother is Mexican," the woman said with pride. "From Guadalajara."

"You should avoid the sun," Edwina told her. "Like me," she said, pulling her fingers away. Touching her cheek to emphasize her point. "You look so . . . foreign."

On the last Sunday of Edwina's life, the sky was pewter. Darla and Teddy sat under the tree, waiting for the rain, singsonging a silly rhyme while popping the heads off dandelions. Edwina pressed her face to the glass as she did when the children played below the window, beneath the tree. Teddy and Darla looked up and waved.

"Why are they always so happy?" she said to the empty room. Their joy rankled her. She did not smile, did not wave. Instead she glowered and continued to watch. She pushed the window up another three inches to better hear what they were saying. Darla picked a dandelion whose head had gone to seed. She closed her eyes, took a deep breath, and blew its flossy fluff into the air. As the seeds scattered, a bunny appeared and hopped across the yard.

"You did it, Darla," Teddy laughed. "Do it again!"

This time a spotted fawn appeared and lowered her head for them to pet.

"You make a wish this time," she said. "I'll blow."

Teddy closed his eyes and made a wish. Darla blew. Ice cream cones appeared in their hands. Three scoops each: vanilla, chocolate, strawberry. "Yay!" Darla said and took a lick of vanilla.

Edwina couldn't stand it—their joy, their laughter.

The tricks her eyes were playing on her.

"Go back to where you came from!" she screamed and stabbed the air with her swollen finger. "Heathens! Chinks!"

114

The last word dropped hard, metallic.

"What's a Chink?" asked Teddy.

"I don't know," said Darla.

"Is that what we are?" asked Teddy. Confusion clouding his question.

"I don't know," said Darla. "I thought we were just us."

Edwina disappeared from her post at the window. When she returned, she leaned out, smashed her giant breasts against the sill, clanged her spoon against the bottom of the pot. Her face plummed purple, her screams pelted. Darla picked a dandelion with a leonine head, and put her thumb on the weed flower's neck. She looked up at Edwina and repeated the rhyme. "Mama had a baby and its head popped off." Darla flicked; Teddy gasped. Together they watched as Edwina's head flew from her body and tumbled through the air. Her mouth still moving, astonishingly silent.

Interlude: Darla

Every year on the anniversary of Edwina Hemplemeyer's death, Teddy and Darla go to the cemetery to lay lilacs on her grave. They never have trouble finding it, because it is the only one covered in a tangle of dandelions and chicken bones sucked mysteriously clean. After Edwina's head popped off, the apartment building was eerily silent. After Edwina's head popped off, Darla's grandma, Vilma, located Edwina's next of kin in Mexico. She invited them to the funeral and they all politely declined. When she asked Edwina's sister if she had an epitaph in mind for the headstone, the woman trilled a quote in rapid-fire Spanish. Vilma asked her to send the words in a letter so she could get the inscription exactly right. Neither Teddy nor Darla—nor Vilma nor Mr. Aikura—knew what it meant until Darla took a trip to Mexico City with her parents in the summer of 1968. There she asked the concierge at their hotel—the Camino Real—to translate the Spanish into English. She laughed so hard that diamonds of salt flew from her eyes.

"Say it again," she said.

"In English?" he asked.

"Spanish and English," she answered.

"En boca cerrada no entran moscas." He smiled, then continued: "In the closed mouth, flies do not enter."

Apartment F: The Radio
(1982)

"What kind of man doesn't want to see his daughter? Get to know his grandchildren?" Elsie wrote to her ex-husband, Warner, when she found out he had been living forty-five minutes away from their daughter in Phoenix. He called Elsie the day her letter arrived. Said she was right, invited her to visit.

"It's been too long," he said. "We'll have steaks and cocktails. We'll dance."

Elsie hasn't seen Warner in forty years. Not since the morning she got on a train with their two-year-old daughter, Astrid, and headed west from her mother-in-law's farm in Wolf Point, Montana, to her father's house in Sandpoint, Idaho. A new town, a new life. Soon she and Warner will be sixty-two-year-old-face to sixty-nine-year-old-face. How, she wonders, will she get through the five-hour drive from Spokane to Helena, the dinner, the night? Every version of it terrifies her. She turns on the transistor radio and hears Patsy Cline singing about faded love. The radio always plays what she needs to hear. She takes a deep breath and another sip of her vodka soda.

In the years that have passed since Elsie last saw Warner, her body has become a war zone: a breast lost to cancer, skin burned by radiation, layers of scar tissue—raised and uneven. Hers is a new topography of skin over bone. When he last saw her, her hair was white blonde, braided, wrapped around her head. Her skin milky and unlined, her teeth white and strong. Now her hair is short and curled, blonde covering gray. One side of her bra foam, her teeth false. Elsie looks in the mirror and pulls her skin toward her ears to tighten it. The face-lift she had four years ago erased ten and made her look more rested. She wishes now that the scalpel had sliced off thirty. She sweeps a sparkle of blue over her eyelids, paints her lips coral, takes another sip of her drink, and considers herself in the mirror. If the light is low, Warner might think she is attractive *for her age*, or better yet, see her as ageless through the prism of nostalgia. She dresses in shades of forest. Her pants are flared, her blouse fitted. She ties a chiffon scarf around her neck, zips up her brown leather ankle boots, slides her Black Hills gold ring onto her finger, the matching earrings into her lobes. She pulls her western tooled-leather purse from the closet, and checks her reflection one more time.

"It's now or never, Elsie," she says into the mirror.

It's almost three o'clock when she pulls her burgundy Olds Toronado onto the I-90 and heads east to Montana. Warner's new-old home. She listens to the radio as she passes through Coeur d'Alene, Kellogg, Wallace, and then to country western

8-track tapes as she drives through a large swath of empty. She reaches Missoula—and, finally, Helena. It is after eight when she pulls into the parking lot of the restaurant. She digs through her purse for a Certs, checks her lipstick in the rearview mirror, and applies another coat. She fluffs the curls around her face. Her heart starts to pound, she has trouble catching her breath, sweat blooms under her arms. She worries her nerves will stain her blouse dark before she gets inside. She worries over what he will think when he sees her. She stands at the entrance to the lounge and looks into the hive of drinkers, sees Warner walking toward her. He's wearing a sky-blue western-yoked shirt, dark slacks, snakeskin cowboy boots. Sharp, she thinks. Handsome still. His once-black hair is salted, his face lined. His eyes bright. His eyes on her.

"Elsie," he says. "Beautiful as ever." He kisses her cheek, puts his hand on the small of her back, guides her to the booth. It's circular and faces out toward the dance floor. He motions for her to go first, slides in beside her, takes her hand in his.

"Warner," she says. She looks down at their hands together—spotted and lined, no longer smooth. "Where do we begin?" She shakes her head and laughs. He orders them each a drink: whiskey neat and a gin and tonic.

"Rocks," Elsie adds.

They two-step politely around the landmines of their long-dead love affair: his infidelity, her anger, his indifference, her sadness. Instead, they talk about her second marriage and his third and fourth. They talk about their daughter, Astrid, her husband, Pascual, and their grandchildren: Pilar, Ander, and Paloma. They talk about Warner's thoroughbreds, his life on the race circuit. After their third cocktail, she says, "I thought you'd follow me, fight for me." Her voice quivers. "I waited," she says. "You never came." He lets this settle. Nods. "I was young, Elsie. Selfish." He takes a drink.

"I'm sorry," he finally says.

After the cocktails, the steaks and potatoes, the shared slice of cherry pie, Warner holds out his hand. "Dance with me," he says. He takes her hand, leads her from the booth to the dance floor, pulls her close. She smells motel soap on his skin, Old Spice. As they dance under the dull bar lights on the small dance floor, life resets: no goodbye, no divorce, no heartbreak. Just him holding her, singing in her ear. They dance while Ferlin sings. Then Merle, Marty, Waylon. Warner tilts Elsie's chin up, says her name, kisses her. Says, "Let's go home, darlin'." Emboldened by gin and a lifetime of regret, she agrees. He finishes his drink, pays the check, leaves a twenty for the waitress.

He tells Elsie that "home" is a motel off the highway. That he only has a house when he has a wife, someone to take care of him. He is a man who only settles down when he tires of his own company, tires of being alone. Otherwise, he is on the road, with his horse, following the race circuit, chasing the next adventure.

"Still a rambling man," she says. He nods and takes one last drag from his cigarette, crushes it into the pavement with the toe of his boot.

She follows him down the under-lit road, loses him at a too-long light. Sees the motel sign—"No Vacancy!" lit up in neon—signals, and moves into the turn lane to make a left into the parking lot. She sees his truck parked in front of his room, the horse trailer parked on the side of the hotel. Knows he is inside turning on the radio, tearing the paper from the motel glasses for a nightcap for the two of them: whiskey and tap water, a shot of his signature charm. The cocktails to be drunk before he seduces her, before he takes her to bed. The traffic passes. She stares at the dark empty road and makes a U-turn, drives west toward Spokane. She can't do it, there is still too much between them. She needs for this night to end on a high note. Hers.

At half past four, the phone rings. "I just walked in the door," she says.

"I've been up all night," says Warner.

"Worried?" she asks. She leans against the wall and unzips one boot and then the other, lets them drop to the floor.

"I have to head down to Santa Anita for a race, but as soon as I get back I'd like to see you again."

She is exhausted by her ten hours on the road, the emotional toll the night has taken on her.

"I don't think so," she says.

"Let me come to you this time," he says. "Please."

"Pilar will be here next week. You can finally meet her."

"I'll see what I can do," he says. "Call you from the road?"

"I won't hold my breath," she says. She tries to laugh easily, but the sound is high and false.

"Elsie?"

"Warner?"

"I love you, darlin'."

She hangs up and cries until the sun comes up over the edge of the eastern sky.

On the nights when Elsie cannot sleep, she turns on her radio and listens to a talk-radio program from San Francisco. The signal so strong it carries seven hundred miles from the station's towers to her Spokane bedroom. The host's voice is molasses, it sweetens her nights, connects her to someone else—even if the connection is one-sided. She's been listening to him since her husband died, since she moved into this South Hill apartment. Five nights a week, for seven years.

On nights when her favorite program isn't on, she turns the

dial until she finds a station that carries over the airwaves from other faraway cities with late-night programming. Sometimes Seattle, sometimes Portland, once Chicago. Never music, only talk. But the talk makes her feel less alone.

Elsie waits idly for Warner's call, the way she has always waited for him. One week bends into two, two into three. He does not call. One afternoon, Pilar catches her staring at the phone, willing it to ring.

"Are you waiting for Warner to call?" she asks.

Elsie looks at Pilar. The girl has the haughty tilt of Elsie's nose, Warner's stare. Strange to see his look of consternation in the set of her fifteen-year-old brow. Elsie wants to tell her no, but she knows Pilar won't believe her, not this girl. Pilar is always listening, always observing.

"I thought he would call," Elsie says. "He said he would call." Now Elsie is the teenager, her crush gone astray.

"Guys never mean what they say, Grandma," Pilar says. Then asks, "Do you have a picture of the two of you? Back then?"

"Let's see what we can find," Elsie says. She motions for Pilar to follow her into the smallest bedroom, which is also her office. She pulls a cardboard box from the closet shelf, then they sit on the floor and pore over the photos. Elsie tells Pilar the story of how she decamped to her father Ruben's house after she left Warner. How she and Astrid moved to

Portland during WWII. How she worked in the laundry of the Kaiser Shipyards to support them. How she hated the work and the wet, dismal city. She tells Pilar stories about Warner—the grandfather the girl has never known, never may know. How he competed in a one-hundred-mile horse race and won. How he looked like a movie star. How she fell in love with him before he even made it across the bar to ask her to dance. How another marriage, two more daughters, another lifetime lived never changed her feelings toward him. How Warner haunted her, was with her, every minute of every day, since the night they met. How their life and love was a country western song, the heartbreak written in from the first line.

Pilar opens a manila envelope filled with black-and-white photographs. The first three are from Elsie's life in Wolf Point: Elsie holding Astrid, Warner holding Astrid, Warner's future third wife—when Elsie was still his second—holding Astrid. All set against the bleak landscape of his mother's eastern Montana farm. Then a series of photos in Sandpoint, of her new life after Warner. She lingers on a photo of herself sitting on the rear bumper of her father's Model T Ford, Astrid in her lap. Her hair is held up in a kerchief, an apron covers her rumpled dress. Her face is unadorned, weary.

"I look exhausted," she says to Pilar. "And so sad."

"You look happy here," Pilar says. "Pretty, too." She hands

a photograph to Elsie. It is of Elsie and her second husband, Harvey, standing in front of one of his taverns on First Avenue in Sandpoint. She looks radiant, content. Was she? Has she misremembered her own life story, her second marriage? She sets the photo aside, holds out her hand for another photo. "It's empty," says Pilar. "There aren't any more." She tips the envelope upside down.

"I don't have a single photo with him," she says. "Not one." The realization streaks through her.

That night Elsie puts old honky-tonk albums on the stereo and turns up the volume. She and Pilar dance in the living room and dining room; they dance down the hall. Pilar sings along, knows the words to all the classics.

"You aren't singing, Grandma," she says. "Why?"

The lung cancer, which came before the breast cancer, took her voice—once melodic, it is now crackly and choppy. *Don't quit your day job*, a date once told her when she forgot herself and sang along to Johnny Cash on the radio. After that, she remembered to sing only when she was alone.

"I lost my voice," Elsie says.

"Not possible," Pilar says and hands her grandma a wooden spoon to use as a microphone.

"Sing with me," she says. Elsie opens her mouth, and the first measure of notes sounds like a croak. Elsie tries again, comes in at a lower octave. They sing one song together and then another. They sing until they are hoarse, until they fall onto the davenport laughing.

Elsie realizes she hasn't sung like this since she and Warner used to sing together in the tavern where they met, where her mother, Alma, worked as a bartender. Where they would harmonize until people put down their beer, stopped their conversations, listened.

After Pilar falls asleep, Elsie lies in bed, replaying her dinner conversation with Warner. Over the past month her memory has taken it from measured and cautious to rapid and discordant. A lifetime of hurt and anger and resentment distilled into a salvo of one liners: You didn't come for me. I waited. You didn't fight for me. *You left me. You didn't say goodbye.* You went out drinking. You left me at home with your mother. *I was young.* You weren't at the hospital when our daughter was born. *I was selfish. You didn't let me see my daughter. You returned my letters unopened.* I brought her to visit. *Once. You brought her once. You remarried! Let another man adopt our daughter.* Eight years later. You remarried two weeks after our divorce. You married someone I hated. *You hated everyone.* Then silence. Then the line that sliced her: You broke my heart.

Between the death of her second husband and the return of

126

the first one, she'd known a string of feckless, irresponsible men. Men who took her out for dinner and dancing. Asked her for money—the money she had inherited from her husband, which all the swindlers knew was a ridiculous amount. Two of them left her branded with embarrassment and shame: the contractor who took her to dinner and made love to her before asking for 40,000 dollars, and the gambler who wore white leisure suits and patent leather shoes, drove a Cadillac, wanted her money to build an addition onto his state-line bar, told her he loved her. Had a wife. When Warner called, she had a faint, foreign feeling—something like hope. Here was her second chance, theirs. She understands that both nothing and everything have changed.

The morning after Pilar flies back to Arizona, Elsie is drinking her first cup of coffee when the phone rings. It's the Helena Police Department.

"A man was found in his hotel room. Your number," the officer says, "was in his wallet." He says Warner's name.

"When?" she asks. "How?"

"Heart attack," he says. "Maid found him yesterday."

She hangs up and takes a sip of coffee, now bitter despite the sugar, the half-and-half. She throws the cup and watches as the tan of the coffee colors the wall.

The Saturday night movie on Channel 2 has ended. It's after

eleven, and Elsie is painfully awake. For over an hour, she twists and turns in the dark quiet of her room. The silence screams, it stirs her insomnia. She reaches over and turns on the radio, turns the dial until she hears the last refrain of an old song she and Warner used to sing together at the tavern where they met. Then, the announcer's voice:

"You are listening to the Saturday night sounds of love and love lost on Wolf Point's own KMGK. As my listeners know, I don't usually take dedications, but tonight I'm making an exception for an old friend. Elsie, this one goes out to you from Warner. He hopes you're listening."

The song is Ferlin's, but the voice is Warner's. He sings about looking sad, about knowing it's over, about life going on. His sugared voice swells in the dark of the room. It's the voice that wooed her into bed, into having his baby, into giving him her heart and never taking it back. The voice that never said goodbye. She leans over, her hand shaking, and turns the radio off before the song ends. Before she hears Warner say, "Elsie, it was always only you."

Interlude: Elsie and Warner

Elsie's radio was last spotted on the shelf in a collectibles shop in Spokane's Garland district. If you are lucky enough to find it, you can turn the dial to the far end to tune into KMGK.

During the day they play Elsie and Warner's favorite songs on repeat; after midnight, if you are fortunate, you may hear them taking over the airwaves in duet.

Apartment G: The Suitcase
(2016)

She arrives at the doorstep of their fading love affair wearing a tomato-red dress and carrying a basil plant that perfumes the air around her.

"For pesto and protection," she says when he opens the door.

"Interesting choice," he says as he takes the plant and ushers her inside.

"Run," she hears the basil say.

"A tour?" he asks. He takes her through his new set of rooms. There are six. In each the boxes are neatly stacked to throat level. Theirs.

"May I help you unpack?" she asks.

"Yes. You start here. And I," he says, pointing in the direction of another room, "will start there."

She opens the first box and finds that it is filled with rage. Red, velvety yards of it. She folds it into squares and tucks it into a dresser drawer. In the next box she finds self-pity. It is squat and rough and withered. She arranges its pieces in a bowl and sets it on the table near the record player. It reminds her of a still life. Dutch. She opens the box marked envy. It flies out and flaps wildly around the room. Tangles in her hair. Another holds a heap of regret, which is dingy and sour. This she tosses into the laundry basket and sets by the door.

She thinks of her own broken emotions, and how they have unnerved all but the most fearless of men: her midnight melancholy that spooked the skateboarder, her volcanic jealousy that perplexed the poet. Then, there was the Thursday in March, when the pregnancy stick twinned pink, and she left the man who planted the truest of loves inside of her. The Friday she drove to her parents' house, pulled her mother's vintage ivory suitcase from a stack in the garage, and crowded it with all of the heartbreak and melancholy she carried from one love to the next. Sent it off to Paris. A one-way ticket. Imagined it being stolen from the luggage carousel of the Charles de Gaulle Airport. Her broken emotions set loose on the streets of the Marais where they could languish in surrealistic splendor. Pout in existential angst. Roam free under gunmetal skies.

She charms and is charmed by men as damaged as birds whose wings have been loosed from their bodies. "Help me," they plead. And she does. She sweeps sadness, hangs self-doubt, slips misplaced dreams into drawers. If their closets or cabinets are full, the broken emotions spill out onto the floor, where they will be stepped over or kicked aside, but never picked up. Never tossed out. As time passed, she would get used to the presence of their broken emotions—accept or ignore them—but as she stares around the room at the stacks of boxes lining the walls, she has an inkling that may never be the case with this particular man.

She unpacks box after box until a wave of exhaustion pushes her onto the bed. Sleeps until he wakes her for dinner.

"Pesto linguine?" she asks. It is her favorite.

"Pot roast and mashed potatoes," he answers. He casts a disparaging glance at her nap-wrinkled dress. "My favorite," he adds.

When she returns the next week, she finds that the basil plant has been stripped of its leaves, and its stalk is drooping.

"Where are its leaves?" she asks.

"I ate them," he answers. "Made pesto linguine."

"Made pesto linguine?" she says confused.

"The basil plant was for me, wasn't it?"

"It was for us," she says, but he doesn't hear her. He is already bent over, sanding the arm of a chair. "Look at this beauty," he says, running a calloused hand over the wood the way he once ran it over her.

She feels faint with disappointment. "I'm not feeling well," she says. "Perhaps I should go."

"Perhaps you should," he says. "I can't afford to be sick. I have work to do."

She steps out the door. "Don't leave me," she hears the basil plant say.

She returns the next Friday and the one after that and the one after that. She unpacks box after box after box. Regardless of how many she empties, she always finds more. When she takes breaks from unpacking, she spins records and fills milk-bread-white pages with loops of black ink. Most of all she wonders if there is any woman he'd put his hammer down for at three o'clock on a Friday afternoon.

Six Fridays pass in this way. Their forty-three hours together become a pattern of predictability. She drives across town, he greets her, he disappears back into his work. She repairs to one of the rooms to unpack. When his day is done, they eat, watch TV, argue, and have unsatisfying sex in the dark among the archeology of his life.

"Why do you keep going back?" her sister asks one Tuesday over pink cake and black tea. "You are settling. And for a pocket-sized man with a colossal ego. A liar. A cheat."

"Loneliness is a strange drug," she says.

"No excuse," her sister says. Then glares at her in that sisterly way she has.

On the seventh Friday, she disappears to a city that spoons a bay called Elliott—where the light dances silver on its surface and alabaster octopi sway in its aqueous depths. In a loft that lies between the water and the tower of a typewriter king, she walks down an ill-lit hallway and falls into an instant-ramen sort of love—fast, satisfying, delicious. He hides his broken emotions under the ink on his skin, the paint he layers onto canvas, but she can see them rippling under the waves of color. Unlike the man hunched over a piece of furniture three hundred miles to the east, he enchants her. His is a heart song she heard before she arrived, before they met.

"You are a gem," he says.

"A cracked pearl," she says. He laughs.

"I'm serious," she says.

The next Friday, she tells the man she does not love that it's time for her to go. As she waits for him to finish his work, she opens the last remaining box. It is labeled: ARTISTIC FAILURE. She slices the tape with a box cutter, pulls open the flaps. Inside she finds scraps of papers scrawled with scorn, a palette crusted with rejection, pages torn from sketch pads filled with frustration, remnants of anguish, the blunted ends of shame. At the bottom lies dented metal tubes of broken emotions. She unscrews the cap of anger and slicks it onto her lips. Catches a glimpse of her reflection in the mirror and feels enlivened by the slash of power it returns to her diminished self. She rims her eyes with lost hope and is astounded by how it illuminates her skin. The sweep of discontent across her lids accents the black of her hair, the brown of her eyes.

After two deadening months with him, she is imbued with flickers and flares and flashes of feeling. She walks into the living room, stands on its edge, says his name.

"We need to talk," she says.

"What is on your face?"

"I opened the last box. There were tubes—" she says.

"How dare you! Those are my possessions and for my use only!"

He turns back to the six o'clock news and leaves her standing there. Ignored. She ignites, flames, threatens to burn. Here is an emotion she remembers from the last time she tried to make their sham of a love affair work—hatred.

Each time a broken emotion landed on her shoulder or tried to ease into her mouth, she brushed it away. Spit it out. Swept it out the door before he could see it. But as her broken emotions became larger, more dense, she dropped them into drawers, hung them in the backs of closets, tucked them behind the spices on the shelf.

She goes back to the bedroom, stands on her tiptoes, pulls a marbled-pink suitcase from the top shelf of the closet. A layer of another woman's self-loathing tumbles down, musses her hair, makes her sneeze.

"Hey, I know you," she says. She opens the suitcase. It smells of dust and is perfumed with anguish, now as faded as the woman who left the suitcase behind. She moves around the apartment opening cabinets and cupboards and drawers, collecting the parts of herself she's secreted away. She arranges and rearranges her collection in the suitcase until it fits. It isn't easy to lift, so she drags it down the hall to the front door.

"I am leaving now," she says.

"Where are you going?" he asks, barely lifting his eyes from the television.

"I'm going away," she says. "For good," she adds.

This gets his attention. The red of him starts to rise. It colors his neck, his ears, the bulb of his nose.

"You? Leaving me?" His voice is fishwife shrill. He looks pointedly at a spot near her feet. "And what is that?"

She follows the line drawn by his eyes. "A suitcase," she says.

"What's in it?" he asks, spittle gathering at the corners of his mouth. "You came without a suitcase. You told me you sent all of your broken emotions to Paris."

"I did. Ages ago. I found this one in the closet," she says. Waves her hand in the direction of the bedroom. "I've gathered so many new ones, I can't possibly carry them all without it."

"I want a woman without a suitcase of broken emotions. I want a woman who doesn't have a suitcase at all. That's why I chose you." He teeters. His arms flail.

She smiles an ersatz smile and begins to drag the suitcase out the front door. The latches pop open and the contents spill out onto the floor: ennui, disappointment, loneliness, humiliation. As she crouches to gather and pack them away, she realizes that, like the woman who left the suitcase behind, she too can leave without it. She need not carry her broken emotions into the future or even beyond the door. They can live with the man who crafted them. Stay where they belong. She steps over the suitcase and out the door. The man's metallic whine follows her down the sidewalk.

"Come back here," he calls.

"Come back," the broken emotions echo. "What about us?"

She doesn't look back, doesn't second-guess her decision. She walks into the deepening blue of twilight. Her arms swinging. Her hands empty. Free.

Interlude: Her

"The troll is trolling," her sister calls and says.

"What?"

"The troll is trolling for women . . . online."

"And you know this how?"

"Intuition and a fake account."

She says her sister's name and laughs. "Since we can't knock him off the bridge into the river, can we pretend that he never existed?"

"Not until you check out his profile." Her phone pings. She opens her sister's text message and enlarges the screenshot. True to his signature style, his profile is an amalgam of half-truths and lies. But the final line, the most revealing of all, is his version of the truth in all its distorted wonder: IF YOU HAVE BAGGAGE, SWIPE LEFT.

Apartment H: The Telephone (2018)

"**B**e back in an hour," Chloe calls out to Stephen. She zips up her bomber jacket, loops a scarf around her neck, tightens her topknot, and steps out the door of the bakery. The sky is silver, and the afternoon smells of wet rocks. *Petrichor,* she once heard it called. Chloe collects facts, stories, and images, and recycles them in her poetry. She walks down Sprague, toward Howard, toward the bookstore. There are days when the shop calls to her, beckons. She listens, knowing that something waits just for her: an old postcard that will spark a new poem, a book that will pull her into the past.

Today, a copy of Erica Jong's *Fear of Flying* catches her eye. She pulls it from the shelf and opens its worn cover. Penned inside in blue ballpoint is a previous owner's name and phone number. She turns the book over. Reads intellectual, reads writer. Reads sex, sex, sex. Reads freedom, reads independence. This is it, the book she is meant to buy.

"Hey, Chloe." It's her neighbor Kaia's son, Ocean Boy, a musician from Seattle, who she's seen on the front steps of Mt. Vernon playing along to country western songs issuing from an old transistor radio: Marty, Merle, Waylon, Ferlin. "Written anything new lately?"

"A line here, a line there," she says.

"I'm playing the Knitting Factory tomorrow night. If you wanna come, I'll put you on the list."

"Maybe," she says. Another guy, another Tuesday. She needs a break from the sameness of her days.

She sits underneath an old black-and-white photograph of a baker (whose sad eyes remind her of Ocean Boy's), standing in front of a towering cake at the Davenport Hotel, and reads the first chapter of her new book. Underlines the phrase *zipless fuck*. Flips to the front of the book and checks the copyright date: 1973. She circles it. Before she leaves to walk back to the bakery, she makes a note on the last page of the first chapter. A reminder: "Less fear, more flying!"

She carries the book with her to and from work. She reads it on break, reads it in bed until she falls asleep. Dreams she lives in 1973 Spokane: a life that is not ordinary, a life that is not tame, a life that is not her own.

She gets to the last chapter of the book, the last page, the last sentence. Wants to talk about what she's read, but who can she call? Stephen is having late-night cocktails at Durkin's with his new love interest, and her grandma—who she is sure read *Fear of Flying* when she was Chloe's age—is asleep in her retirement community on the other side of the country.

142

Then it hits her. She'll call Helen, the woman whose book she bought. Anyone who writes their name and phone number in a book claims it. Wants it back if it's lost in a coffee shop or on a bus. She picks up the receiver of the mid-century, aqua-blue rotary phone she purchased at a collectibles shop on Market Street.

"This baby has magic left in her yet," the old man told her when she bought it.

She dials the number, realizes she forgot the area code. Starts to press the switch hook to end the call, but hears it ring—once, twice. What happens if Helen doesn't pick up? Should she leave a message? A woman answers.

"Helen?" Chloe asks. "Helen Moore?"

"Yes," Helen says.

"I was wondering—" Chloe starts. Realizes she has no idea what to say. "Have you read *Fear of Flying?*"

"Are you from the Book of the Month Club?"

"No, I bought your copy of the book at a used bookstore? Your name and number are in it."

"Damn it. I let Connie borrow it and she never returned it. Now I know why."

They talk for the next hour. Helen says things like *foxy* and *boogie*. Tells Chloe she lives in an old SRO hotel on First Avenue—hot plate and sink in her room, bathroom down the hall. She wants to be an artist, but for now she works in the dietary department of Sacred Heart Hospital making vitamin shakes and delivering meals to patients. Her unofficial title: *Nutrition Girl.* She tells Chloe she survives on a diet of Kool cigarettes and Sanka instant coffee. "Decaf," she says, "with half-and-half and Sweet'N Low." *Cosmo* is her bible. She drives a red VW Bug. She's twenty-three, a Capricorn. Chloe finds her captivating, enchanting. Helen might be the most rad woman she's ever talked to. She likes things that Chloe has never even considered. Like Funk. Like the poems of Rod McKuen. Like wanting to live in San Francisco.

Chloe calls Helen every Sunday night at seven. They talk about Gloria Steinem. They talk about Roe v. Wade. They talk about AIM and the Occupation of Wounded Knee. Chloe tries to talk about the Dakota Pipeline, but Helen keeps correcting. "You mean Alaska?"

Chloe tells Helen that she went on a date with a guy she didn't really like because she didn't know how to say no. He took her to Ferguson's. Ate French fries with his mouth open. Talked at her. Halfway through her huckleberry milkshake, she feigned a migraine. Asked for a rain check on the movie they were supposed to see at the Garland Theater. As he drove up Monroe toward the South Hill, toward Tenth, he looked over at her and said, "I can still come in, right?"

Helen says her new boyfriend's name: first, middle, last, and suffix—all beginning with J. She tells her how they went dancing and got drunk on Harvey Wallbangers and Golden Cadillacs. How they had sex in his car on the PINK level of the Parkade. Got locked in the parking garage and had to climb over a wall to get out. Helen in her pointelle minidress and platforms. Johnny in his polyester dress shirt, high-waisted bell bottoms, and platforms. He lost his fedora, she lost a bangle.

Chloe knows she's giving seven-eighths of herself to her friendship with Helen, but except for Stephen, her coworker at the bakery, she is alone in this town. She left her family in New Jersey (mom, dad, brother, grandma) and came to Spokane to study poetry at Eastern. After graduation, her friends moved away, and she stayed. Before Helen, she didn't have one friend who wasn't Stephen. He takes care of her in small but important ways. When she's sad, he makes her laugh. When she's tired, he makes her a double espresso. When she's lonely, he waits until the shop is empty, then turns the music up and dances with her until she forgets.

Chloe rents *Cinderella Liberty*. Calls Helen to tell her she watched it.

"What a trip to see Pike Place Market in 197—" Chloe starts.

"He got fired today," Helen interrupts. "It's all my fault."

"Who?" Chloe asks and bites the chocolate frosting peak

from her cupcake.

"Johnny, Chloe. Johnny got fired." Helen starts to cry. Hard.

What Chloe gets is that someone saw Helen and Johnny together, outside of work, on a date. Their opposite ends of the spectrum skin is unacceptable to many in this town, even now. It is the reason for his dismissal. He knows it and she knows it. The hospital invents an infraction, but all who know him say he's the best cook on the line. Chloe hears knocking.

"Can I call you right back?" Helen says. "There's someone at the door."

Chloe waits. Ten minutes turn to thirty, a half hour to an hour. Her phone doesn't ring. She dials Helen's number at the sixty-minute mark.

"Chloe?" Helen says. "Is that you?"

"It's me," Chloe says.

"Thank God! I tried calling you back, but it wouldn't connect. I even called the operator and asked her to try. She said your number doesn't exist. But here you are, so she was wrong." They laugh over the woman's blunder.

"You good?" Chloe asks.

"I ran downstairs to Handy Mart and got a TaB. Then I smoked a joint." Helen laughs as a way of finishing her sentence, of answering Chloe's question. "What were we talking about?" Helen asks.

"Johnny," Chloe reminds.

"It was Johnny at the door. He's here. Johnny, say hi to Chloe."

"Hey Chloe, how's it going?" she hears him holler.

"Hi Johnny," Chloe hollers back through the line.

"Johnny and I were talking about what happened. It's a civil rights violation. He's going to call Carl Maxey. See if he'll take the case."

"Carl Maxey?" says Chloe.

"You've heard the saying, 'Take it to Carl,' right? Him."

"Yeah, totally," says Chloe. But Chloe doesn't know who Carl Maxey is, and she doesn't want to ask. She wants Helen to think she is informed. Chloe writes "CARL MAXEY" in her spiral notebook. Circles it three times.

"Do I ever get to meet my replacement?" Stephen asks Chloe one morning as they are opening the shop.

"Yes, but I have to meet her first," says Chloe.

"Is she even real?" Stephen laughs.

"Of course she's real," says Chloe. "We just work opposite hours. When I'm working, she's sleeping, and vice versa."

Stephen looks at her. "Not real," he says and pulls an errant strand of hair that has slipped from her topknot.

"Don't be mean," she says.

The second thing Helen says to Chloe after *hello* is: "I switched shifts and got tomorrow off. We can finally hang out. Meet me under the clock at the Crescent? One o'clock?"

"How will I know it's you?" Chloe asks.

"I'm a dead ringer for Sally Struthers," Helen says.

"Sally Struthers?" says Chloe. Writes the name on a scrap of paper.

"You crack me up, Chloe! You do watch TV, don't you?" Helen laughs. "What about you?"

Chloe thinks about reruns she has watched on late-night television with her grandma. Remembers *The Mary Tyler Moore Show*. Remembers Rhoda. "Rhoda," she says.

"Perfect, see you tomorrow, Rhoda. One o'clock. Don't forget about the Christmas crowds. Keep your eyes peeled so you don't miss me."

Chloe arrives early. Brings two coffees and Helen's copy of *Fear of Flying*. Under Helen's name and phone number, she's added line drawings of cigarettes, coffee cups, butterflies, daisies. Things that remind her of Helen. There is no one in the Crescent Court. Why, she wonders, did Helen suggest they meet in this corporate, vanilla wasteland? And then Chloe notices the lingering ghosts of the department store that once occupied this space: the twin, stacked clocks hanging from the ceiling, the escalator, the bank of elevators, the metalwork balcony with its decorative crescent moons, the five steps that lead to a wall covered with fake green foliage and a concrete title block in the middle of it that reads: CRESCENT. She goes up and down the escalator, then takes the elevator to the second floor and peers over the railing into the boring block of space below. Finally, she sits on the bottom step, below the wall of green, and watches as the long hand of the clock moves from three to six to nine. Helen doesn't come. Chloe calls her as soon as she gets home.

"You didn't come," she says, when Helen answers the phone.

"I did. I waited. There were so many people," says Helen.

"Helen, no one was there," Chloe says. Her voice edged with sadness.

"Chloe, what are you talking about?"

Chloe hunts for albums Helen listens to. Searches for sitcoms Helen talks about watching on her rent-to-own black-and-white TV. Scours thrift stores looking for a fur to throw over her maxi-slip dress and cognac, knee-high leather boots. She wants to go dancing. She wants have sex with everyone. She wants to say yes to everything. She wants to devour the world.

Stephen teases her about her free fall into the 1970s. Her refusal to engage with technology. "Time to come into the twenty-first century, Chloe," he says.

"I think I'm fine right where I am," she answers. He hands her an Americano. Black. Watches as she pours in a double shot of cream and a stream of sugar.

"New drink?" he asks.

"New me," she answers.

One night Chloe gets drunk on a wicker-wrapped bottle of chianti. She turns up the volume on the *Sly and the Family Stone* album and dances around her apartment in her bra and panties and new-old fur coat. The one with a label that reads: "B. Furriers, Spokane, WA." She wants to call Helen to tell her about a girl who came into the bakery and asked her out for cocktails tomorrow night. She wants to be bolder in her choices, braver. She wants to be like Helen. She dials Helen's number and gets a busy signal. She drinks and spins, spins and drinks, and with each spin the phone cord wraps more tightly around her. She laughs at how her life is coming together in the most unexpected way. She trips and stumbles over a stack of books, and rips the cord out of the wall. The phone clatters to the floor, the dialer cracks. Chloe watches as a triangle of it hits the baseboard. She plugs it back in and listens. There is only silence. She hits the switch hook again and again, dials the unbroken zero for the operator. Screams into the dead receiver.

A week passes, then two. Her grandma buys her a new phone to replace the old one. "It's smart," she tells her. Chloe pecks Helen's number onto the screen. Unlike the old phone, it

won't connect without the area code. She tries again. Hits
5-0-9. A man answers.

"Is Helen there?" she asks.

"Wrong number," he says and hangs up.

She calls again. The same man answers. She tries a different
approach. "Johnny? Is this Johnny? May I speak to Helen?"

"I don't know who Johnny is—or Helen." He hangs up
again.

She tries one more time. "Please don't hang up," she says.
Repeats Helen's number to the man who is not Johnny. Does
not know Helen. Right number, wrong person.

"I've had this number for over forty years," he says, "Don't
call here again."

"But Helen," she says to no one.

She tries a few times after that, usually from the bakery,
but her calls all go to voicemail. She hears his name, Helen's
number. She doesn't understand.

Months stack on top of each other. Chloe goes back to
drinking Americanos. Black. Stops writing poems. Listens to
Lana Del Rey's *Lust for Life* on repeat. Gets high more than
she should, drinks too much wine. Goes on dates with men
and women she has no interest in—has sex she does not feel.
Promiscuity, she decides, is exhausting.

Chloe comes to work with the lavender smudges of insomnia

beneath her eyes. Stephen pulls a shot of espresso, adds water, hands it to her.

"After work, we're going to find her," he says. "You know where she lives, right?"

She nods. "An old single room occupancy hotel on First and Madison," she says. She leans into him, her version of a hug, puts her head on his shoulder.

"You're the best non-boyfriend a girl could ever ask for," she says.

At nine, Chloe and Stephen close the shop and walk down First. Past the Ridpath (where, she tells Stephen, Elvis stayed— twice); the Davenport, Towers and Historic (where Sammy Davis Jr. tried to stay, but a room was denied, a racial slur was hurled, and a punch was thrown that broke the singer's nose); the twin stacks of the Steam Plant lit up in purple; the Fox Theater (where a worker named Otis fell from a scaffolding to his death and lives on as the resident ghost). When they arrive at Madison, Chloe points down the street to the old Union Bus Depot and tells Stephen that was where Jack Kerouac got off the bus one snowy Sunday afternoon and walked down Sprague to the Great Northern Depot. Stephen pushes her pointed finger down and laughs, "Stop with the stories, Miss Spokane; we have a friend to find." The hotel's unlit neon sign is anchored to the eastern corner of the building; on the First Avenue side, there is a sign that reads: *Restaurant Open 24 Hours, Carriage Room.* Helen had mentioned a fourth-floor room, Madison side. Helen had mentioned eating late-night plates of pancakes at the Coach House after dancing, and having cocktails in the Carriage Room. What she hadn't mentioned were the boarded-up windows or the chain-link fence hugging the building. The fact that the hotel is dark—abandoned.

"Are you sure we have the right building?" Stephen asks, his voice drenched in doubt. He does not repeat his belief that Helen is not real, does not voice his fear that his friend may be losing her mind, but Chloe knows he's thinking it.

"Positive," Chloe says. The night is warm, but icy fingers of uncertainty trace her spine.

Chloe tries to let the idea of Helen go, but—real or imagined— how do you forget a person who is the thread that colors your world, rebinds you? She keeps the broken, blue phone on her desk as a reminder of their friendship, the spiral notebook that holds the scribbles she made during their calls.

On her break one afternoon, Chloe walks to the bookstore, and there on the shelf is a biography of Carl Maxey. It reminds her of Helen, so she buys it and sits down with a coffee to skim through it. She learns that Maxey was the first African American to graduate from Gonzaga and practice law in

Spokane; she learns that he fought against prejudice and injustice in a time when others kept quiet, she learns that he died by his own hand, at the age of seventy-three—in 1997. Over twenty years ago! She texts Stephen and tells him she has to go home. "An emergency," she says. She takes a taxi up the hill to her apartment. "Keep the meter running," she tells the driver. She runs upstairs and riffles through her notebook until she finds Carl Maxey's name written in hot-pink ink and circled three times. She grabs it and the telephone and shoves them into her Get Lit! tote bag. Why did Helen talk about Carl Maxey in the present tense? She needs answers. If she can't get them from Helen, she will try to get them from the man who sold her the phone. He knows something, and she needs to know what it is.

When the taxi pulls up to the Hillyard address she's given the driver, she finds a tavern where the collectibles shop once stood. Maybe someone there can tell her where the old man and his shop went. She takes a seat at the end of the bar and orders a Harvey Wallbanger. The bartender brings her a tallboy of Rainier. "On the house," he says after he cracks open the can for her.

"Wait," she says. "The collectibles shop that was here before the bar, where did it go?"

"Can't say. The bar's been here for the last seven years, and before that it was a barber shop." She downs her beer, goes outside, vomits into the sunshine-soaked gutter, then calls another taxi to take her back up the hill.

One March morning, a woman comes into the bakery. Older, tiny, dominoing into seventy. She has platinum hair—short and spiked—and smells of jasmine and cigarette smoke; her nails are painted clay brown. Cool color, thinks Chloe. So '70s. The woman asks Chloe cupcake questions; her voice is throaty, familiar.

"Have we met?" Chloe asks.

The woman looks at Chloe's sky-blue, scoop-neck *Expo'74* tee, the fade of her bell-bottom jeans, the gold hoops dangling from her ears. She leans in and smells her perfume. Musk. "Did you raid your grandmother's closet?" she asks. Chloe laughs. "A friend's influence," she says. The woman orders a Tuesday flavor: a vanilla cupcake with pink frosting. Adds a small decaf coffee, with half-and-half and a packet of Sweet'N Low. Hands Chloe her credit card and drops a folded dollar bill into the tip jar. Chloe traces the name on the card and pales.

"Helen?" Chloe asks. "Helen Moore?" The woman nods.

"Have you ever read *Fear of Flying?*" Chloe asks.

Helen looks at Chloe as if she's mad as a hatter. "We all read it," she says, " . . . in 1973." She glances at the cup of coffee Stephen has set on the counter. Chloe can tell Helen is losing her patience as fast as the coffee is losing its steam. Chloe presses on.

"Do you know Chloe Mazar?" she asks.

Confusion zigzags over Helen's face. "I did, decades ago."
She pauses. "And then one day, she disappeared." She snaps
her fingers. "Just like that."

Chloe shakes her head, reaches across the counter, and
puts her hand on Helen's arm.

"No, Helen," she says. "I didn't."

Helen's eyes narrow and drink Chloe in. Her skin that sings
the song of the Mediterranean sea, mascaraed doe eyes, coffee-
bean hair pulled into a messy topknot. Her undone beauty.

"Holy shit!" Helen says. "Rhoda! It's you."

Interlude: Chloe

Spotted on Chloe's refrigerator (next to a review by Erica Jong of Chloe's award-winning collection inspired by Fear of Flying *and her out-of-time friendship with Helen) is a vintage postcard—postmarked April 4, 1917. A prompt for a new series of poems:* Found Love. *On the front is a tinted illustration of the Eiffel Tower, on the back a message written in mesmerizing loops of black ink. It reads:*

DEAR EMIL,

TOMORROW I AM BEING SENT TO THE FRONT, BUT TONIGHT I AM DRINKING ABSINTHE—FITTINGLY KNOWN AS THE GREEN FAIRY—IN THE SHADOW OF THIS GRAND EDIFICE (SEE FRONT) AND REPLAYING OUR PARTING WORDS TO EACH OTHER AT THE SILVER GRILL. I WAS WRONG, FORGIVE ME. IF I DON'T MAKE IT BACK TO SPOKANE, I WANT YOU TO KNOW TWO THINGS: WITH YOU I AM WHOLE, WITHOUT YOU—I AM A CONSTELLATION OF SCARS.

YOURS, THOMAS

Apartment I: The Fugu
(2018)

Late one night, before summer turned to fall, Ocean Boy was born in a desert town at the confluence of two mythic rivers. He was descended from men who dove for pearls in the waters of a faraway Pacific archipelago, fished the deep waters off the coast of the city named after a saint. His mother was a girl who could dive deeper and swim faster than the boys of her one-time coastal town. *A mermaid,* the kind ones called her. *Bottom dweller,* the unkind ones said.

As he grew from a boy to a man, he played the guitar to keep the demons of despair that haunted him at bay. Wrote songs of longing for a place that sang to him as he slept. Plaintive, baleful songs soaked with melancholy. Songs of the deepest blue. But here, in this town at river's edge—where the winds were fierce and dust could blind—his songs fell on ears that could not hear the rhythm of the ocean written into them.

Ocean Boy started to spin in the chaos of winds called Termination. He could not breathe. The doctors called it asthma, but his mother knew it was sickness for the home he had not yet found. The one that saturated his songs, him.

The days passed and the music that once flooded him stopped.

Perplexed by the loss of his lifelong companion, he put down his guitar and called his mom.

"I can't hear anything but the wind. The music is gone," he said. "Dead. Who am I without it?"

"You are your music," she said.

"Exactly," he said.

He thought of his grandpa, who lived and died because of these winds, this town, that power plant. The winds blew men off the job site: away from home, away from marriages, away from children. The leaving winds. His grandpa had chosen to stay.

"I gave everything to that company," he would remind Ocean Boy. The edges of his grandpa glowed green when the sun set. Ocean Boy wondered if death was scripted into his own DNA—like his grandpa, because of his grandpa?

Ocean Boy moved to the city that was emerald. Went to work in a restaurant in Nihonmachi owned by a childhood friend of his grandpa's. Washed dishes until the old man pulled him into the kitchen.

"Enough," he said one night. Instead, he trained him to slice vegetables, cut fish, hand press vinegar rice. Ocean Boy took pride in his work. He wanted to prove himself, show the old man he could do it—for himself and his grandpa. He practiced, perfected.

"Very good, very good," the old man praised.

On days when Ocean Boy didn't work, he wandered the streets of his neighborhood. He liked that it was once known as the Lava Beds. Thought it fitting since his family hailed from a strand of islands with one hundred volcanoes. He also liked that these blocks were once the center of the city's vice and sin—brothels, box houses, saloons, and gambling halls—which, he thought, always made a place more interesting. He drank beer in a tavern with one hundred years of sordid stories soaked into its floorboards, ate tacos on a patio facing an alley filled with art and bantered with a beautiful server named after a song, searched for ghost signs on the sides of old brick buildings. Sometimes, he sat under the viaduct and smoked cigarettes as he watched the late afternoon light flirt with the water of Elliott Bay.

"Sit," the old man said one night after the restaurant emptied. "Tonight, we celebrate Ebisu, the happy god of children, fish, and fortune. I'm going to make you something special."

He pulled up his sleeve, chased a blowfish with a net, scooped it from the tank. Leaned in and said something to it. Quickly and deftly moved his knife through the fish until it became whispers of sea flesh mounded on a plate with white radish and green citrus. He poured cold rice wine into a cup, pushed it across the short expanse of glass. Raised his own bottle of beer to Ocean Boy.

"Kanpai!" each said to the other.

"What did you say to him?" asked Ocean Boy. The old man laughed, "I told him not to kill you. Fugu is deadly if not cut correctly."

Five nights a week, Ocean Boy and the old man sat on crates in the alley and smoked cigarettes. Sometimes they talked, sometimes they sat in silence. The old man looked forward to this time, and so did Ocean Boy. These times always began with small talk. *What did you do on your day off? Have you tried the malasadas at Fuji? The barbecued pork at Tai Tung? Did you catch the game last night? The news?* Once Ocean Boy tried to ask the old man about his time working side by side with his parents in the fields of the Sacramento Delta, his childhood internment at Topaz. Two particular things he knew about his companion.

"Forgotten time," the old man said. But Ocean Boy knew a childhood sliced in two by toil and war was not forgotten.

"Tell me your stories," the old man said. So Ocean Boy did.

Ocean Boy told the story of how he grew up in a loving, left-of-center family, with his mom, his grandma and grandpa, an auntie, two uncles. How food and laughter were their religion. How beyond their small circle, life was a series of small and large cruelties that, over time, became tidal, threatened to drown. How the neighborhood children called him *Whale*. A single word taunt stuck on repeat, followed by peals of laughter that shadowed him to the cafeteria, the gym, the library. When he was older and the roundness of childhood had dropped away, the jibe turned to *Thinks he's Neptune*, sneered with derision. How his grandpa had died before he had taught Ocean Boy how to be a man. Before they had gotten to take long road trips together, eaten burgers at roadside stands, inked winning numbers onto Keno paper. "We'll win big," his grandpa would say. "Move to the islands. I'll paint and you can play music. We can fish and go kaukau." But the poison that was nuclear took him too soon.

Ocean Boy told the old man how his father—whose ancestors came from an island in a sea where selkies swam—had left him behind. Set off to the Rose City to make the dreams of a girl, not much older than Ocean Boy, come true. When their ill-fated love affair reached its expiration date, Ocean Boy's father was lured in by a woman of the land: tall and strong and thick as the trees that lined the shores of the river that cut their metropolis in two. Ocean Boy became a footnote in his father's story, forgotten when the new wife had one child, then two. Erased.

Ocean Boy described how he put down his guitar when a sound void hit him like a tsunami. How he was assailed with an unfathomable loneliness for a place he could not name. The old man knew no advice could ease the deep ache of a life disrupted by cruelty, the inhumanity of others. He let the boy talk, and he listened.

Weeks passed. Ocean Boy's memories got louder, started to loop. A sudden swell of sadness overtook him. The oceanic one he had inherited from his mother and his grandfather. The cruel voices of the past became a reprise.

One night he touched the center of his bottom lip with the tip of the knife used to prepare the blowfish. His lip tingled, numbed. A week later, he touched the knife to the tip of his tongue. The sensation was more intense: tingle, numb, float. He repeated this practice nightly. Let the knife rest longer. The fleeting thrill became a need.

Days bent into months. Ocean Boy died small deaths daily, heart cell by heart cell. The blowfish poison dulled the pain, dulled his dreams. At night, he fell into a chasm of black slumber or didn't sleep at all. He became disoriented, vacant, a ghost.

On nights he didn't put the fugu knife to his lips, he'd wake the next morning with the taste of sugar and pineapple on his tongue. On the days when there was a respite from the thrum of rain inside his head, and the static of sadness went silent, he could hear the mele of the islands. *Come home*, they sang.

As the months collected into a year, Ocean Boy devoted his life to fugu. At work, he watched the blowfish swim in their tank, whispered kind words before he took their lives, sliced them, served them. At midnight, he walked down Jackson to his apartment that sat in the night glow of Smith Tower. Turned the TV on and the sound down, opened the foil packet that held the fugu liver stolen from the restaurant, shaved off a piece with the hand-forged knife he bought from the kitchen store at Pike Place Market, lifted it with chopsticks, placed it on his tongue, waited for the poison to surge through him.

The rush of euphoria built until he thrashed and flailed, hit his head on the countertop and the underside of the cupboards, tore at the skin he wanted to escape until blood painted his nails. He gasped for air, his movements slowed, his eyes clouded. Finally, he fell into the chair in front of the mute television, his nightly ritual complete. He had become the fugu. Pulled from his tank, slapped onto the counter, skinned and sliced, devoured.

Late one November night, the old man put his hand on Ocean Boy's wrist. Pressed it into the cutting board before he could lift the knife to his tongue.

"I can't stop," Ocean Boy said.

The old man took the knife from his hand. "You're drowning. It's time to go." He reached into the pocket of his worn, blue work coat, and pulled out a ticket. Printed in black was the name of the island of Ocean Boy's grandpa, his great-grandpa. Ocean Boy shook his head. "It's too much!" he said.

The old man motioned to the other side of the counter, then joined him. "Let me tell you a story," he said.

"When your grandpa and I were little, we went to a school for Chinese, Japanese, and Filipinos only. No white kids. They had their own school. Then Pearl Harbor was bombed, and we Japanese were sent to the camps. Half the children and teachers from our school disappeared, so it closed. Your grandpa and all of the others who were left were sent to the other school, the white one. When I came back after the war, the kids made my life hell—they spit on me, called me names, beat me up—even the ones I grew up with in the pear orchards and the asparagus fields. They didn't want to be close to me for fear that my misfortune was contagious. But not your grandpa. He put up his fists and fought for me. We were eleven years old. He did that for me; I want to do this for you."

It was the most the old man had ever shared. "Take it," he said. "Please." Ocean Boy hugged the old man and cried into the blue of his coat.

That night, Ocean Boy packed his waterside life into two duffle bags, then called his mother.

"I get in before daybreak," he said. He got on a midnight bus and headed east across the state to Spokane. Stared at his reflection in the black of the window. He was a stranger, even to himself. His mother arrived early, but the bus arrived earlier. She circled the inside of the depot but could not find her son. On her third orbit, she stopped in front of a man: bearded, gaunt, haunted, lips cracked, a gash caked with blood over his right eyebrow.

"Ocean Boy?"

"Mama!"

In a decades-old diner on Garland, over eggs and toast, Ocean Boy described his daily escape to her as diving into blue and staying under until the moment before surrendering to the silence. But before the dive, there was the excitement that preceded the slice of body into water: the shiver, the sting, the surge.

"I'm sorry I'm so broken," he said. Salt collected on his cheekbones and hers.

A string of weeks later, he picked up his guitar, blew the dust from its neck, strummed until it became a melody. His unused voice cracked. He took a breath, reached into the hidden place inside of himself that the sadness hadn't touched. His voice grew, regained, redoubled. His mother watched as his facade of false bravado shattered and fell to the floor.

"You're back," she said. Her voice flooded with astonishment.

"I'm back," he said. Leaned his guitar against the wall. "But where did I go?" he asked. His seawater eyes alight with wonder. "Why didn't you save me?"

"I tried. Only you could save you."

Night after night, Ocean Boy heard a faraway song as he slept. A sugared voice, a ukulele. When he opened his eyes the last notes of the song were fading as the sun pushed over the edge of the eastern sky.

One December morning, Ocean Boy stood with his mother in their Inland Empire airport, not wanting to say goodbye. She pulled at her lower lip with her teeth. He knew she was trying to keep from crying. To keep from saying the things she really wanted to say, like, *Don't go.*

"Last call for Flight 173," the announcement overhead bellowed.

"That's me, Mama. I've gotta go or I'll miss the plane," he said.

"I know," she said in a voice so small it sounded like a child's.

He picked up his bag and his guitar, then leaned down

and kissed her forehead. When he turned around to holler a final farewell, he saw a wave of tears crash against her ankles.

Ocean Boy flew over the blue expanse of sea. When he arrived on the island, he checked into a hotel where Elvis stayed. This he did for his mother. He walked the streets of Chinatown. This he did for his great-grandpa. He ate burgers and fished from an old seawall. This he did for his grandpa. He sat on the beach, played his guitar, listened to the waves argue with the sand. This he did for himself. He rented a Jeep and drove around the island. Made up stories of what his time with his grandpa would have looked like here. Stopped at places they should have seen together: the base where his grandpa was once stationed, the dock where his great-grandpa got off the boat from another island, the now empty buildings where his mom used to buy shave ice and crack seed. Small histories that made up a larger one—his.

On the day before he was scheduled to fly back to the mainland, Ocean Boy stopped at a diner for eggs and rice. After he had eaten and paid the check, he stood in the parking lot and smoked a cigarette. Let the island's chords wash over him. The multisyllabic crash of the waves, the whisper and sigh of the palm trees, the velvet-winged flap of the wind, the soft-shoe rhythms of the late morning rain. It was, he realized, the sound of home.

Interlude: Kaia

Ocean Boy's mom pulls a sky-blue envelope from her mail slot in the foyer. She slides her finger under the flap and tears it open. Inside is a 1970s-inspired save the date announcement:

YOU'RE INVITED

—TO CELEBRATE—

THE WEDDING OF

CHLOE

&

OCEAN BOY

SATURDAY 8 FEBRUARY

HONOLULU, HAWAII

STARTING AT 7 P.M.

Apartment J: The Mirror
(1914—2024)

And if he left off dreaming about you, where do you suppose you'd be?

—Lewis Carroll

THE MIRROR MAKER

In Germany, we have a story that tells of a magic mirror. The tale is one my mother told me on winter nights when I could not sleep and wanted her close—even though her words made me shiver more than the boreal blackness of our Bavarian village. The legend is one that I carried across the ocean with me to this strange and foreign place called Spokane. It is the reason I began painting silver onto glass for a living. *Mirrors can transport us through time*, my Mutti used to say. *They can also lock us in time.* This is the reason mirrors must be covered at night when we dream, when our souls travel. We should never sleep with them too close to our beds or even within view. An uncovered mirror invites the traveling spirits to peek at us while we are sleeping. Speak to us. And if we aren't careful, try to pull us through it to the other side.

IRIS

"Everyone, everyone," the photographer hollers above the din. Iris glances down from her seat on the balcony to where Mr. Libby has set up his camera at the front of the hall. No one is paying attention. His photograph will have to capture everyone as they are, in various states of inebriation and flirtation. Champagne spilling onto the floor, hair coming undone, ties and lips loosened. Iris watches as Mrs.— dramatically bats her eyelashes at a man not her husband. Mr.— runs his finger down the arm of a man he has just met, while the local gossip has his wife's ear. Miss— pulls on the bodice of her dress as if overcome by an August heatwave, while her escort tips into her breasts in a humid swoon. The flash goes off and for a moment the room falls silent. Iris leaves the torpid, smoke-heavy ballroom and goes downstairs to stand on the mezzanine. She watches the dancers in the lobby circle the fountain crowded with dark red roses, watches as members of the Blackfeet Tribe—dressed in white buckskin and white feathers—mingle with the guests. Alabaster birds in a room filled with ravens. Her husband, Joseph, finds her in the swell of merrymakers.

"There you are," he says. "I've been looking for you everywhere."

"It's like the Mad Hatter's Tea Party in there," she says, motioning toward the ballroom. He laughs. "Here you are, *Alice.*" He hands her a plate with a triangle of cake. It's stacked and seamed with huckleberry.

"How did you know I was starving?" she says.

"Because, Liebling, you are always starving." A waiter passes. Joseph takes two glasses of champagne and hands one to her. "Prost to you, my darling. To lifetimes." They raise their glasses.

"To lifetimes," she says and takes a sip. A flash goes off as he leans forward to tuck a strand of hair behind her ear.

"Beautiful," Mr. Libby says, as he looks over the top of his camera at them. "A photo for the ages."

(Opening Night Party, The Davenport Hotel,
September 19, 1914)

JOSEPH

Joseph pours three fingers of whiskey into a glass and shakes sleeping pills from the cardboard pill box onto his desk. He lines them up into three neat rows of ten. Swallows them—one, two, five at a time. Takes the final sip of whiskey, leans back in his chair, and closes his eyes. He thinks of Iris: marrying her on a December night in the Hall of Doges, while outside the crushed-diamond sky competed with the Christmas lights that lined Riverside Avenue; their transcontinental adventures to Manhattan—the city where he grew up, became a man; Sunday afternoons spent lying on their blue, velvet davenport, reading, drinking basement-pressed red wine (made by their neighbor, the man everyone calls the *bachelor baker*) and listening to Bing Crosby on the phonograph. He loves her madly, his Iris. Her life, he thinks, will be easier without him and his midnight moods. He will no longer dull the sizzle and pop of her personality. He begins to feel the downward pull of the pills. A wash of panic floods him. What has he done? "Iris!" he hollers. There is a flash of arctic white. And silence.

(June 1931)

THE ACTOR

Spokane. What can I say? It's a strange and beautiful place— with its low-slung, brick buildings and evergreen trees, its fairytale towers and wild river that cuts through the middle of the city. Today the crew is shooting the final scene at Mt. Vernon Apartments on the South Hill. I can tell it used to be really something back in the day, but now it just looks worn and tired. I watched as the crew pulled the royal-blue, wool carpet up and put down one that is beige and thin and seems out of place in the faded grandeur of the building. They steamed off the wallpaper too. Strip after flocked, blue strip. What a waste. New isn't better. New doesn't hold history. It doesn't hold stories with weight. I wander around outside as they arrange the set for the day's shoot, and find an old coal bin on the side of the house, the shell of an elevator in the basement. I get into it, close the door, turn the lever in one direction and then the other. It doesn't move. I go back up

174

the stairs and through the empty halls, I try the doors. Most are locked, but the last door opens.

"Hello," I call. "Anyone here?" There's furniture, but it's covered with sheets, and like everything else it looks like it hasn't been used for years. Decades. I walk from room to room, lifting the drop cloths, imagining how impressive the apartment must have been in its heyday: oak floors; a worn, blue velvet couch; a pink bathtub; remnants of an all-white turn-of-the century kitchen, with an icebox and flour bin; a sunroom down a long hall with a built-in wardrobe, its curtains long gone, but its pale pink edges wink—invite a second look. The room next to it has a black, Art Deco bed and a dresser. I pull the sheet from the mirror above it and startle myself with my own reflection. In my high-waisted black trousers and coattails, I look like I belong in this room, this apartment, back when it was new and occupied by people from another era. I open the dresser drawers one by one; each is empty. In the last one, I see the top edge of an old photograph. I pull it out. It is creased and faded. An image of a dark-haired woman and a dark-haired man. I trace the woman's face in the photograph. She is laughing. Her hair is pulled up and pinned; her eyebrows are strong, her nose prominent, her lips full. The man, in a black top hat and tails, leans toward her, his face slightly blurred. Even out of focus, I can see that he looks like me. Weird, I think. I turn it over and read the handwritten script: "Joseph and Iris Mann. September 19,

1914." The photographer's name, Charles Libby, is stamped on the bottom.

The heat in the room and the wool of the costume are soporific. Well, that and the pot I smoked with one of the grips after shooting the last scene. I slip the photo into the pocket of my coat, lie down on the bed, and close my eyes. Almost immediately, I see the woman from the photo, here in this room, leaning toward the mirror, her face covered in cold cream. "Iris?" I say. "Joseph?" she says and then fades out. Then I see a woman I recognize standing in the doorway. I hear the word *ice cream*, the word *huckleberry*. Can she see me? I wave just as she turns. Then she, too, is gone. Finally, I see a girl of a woman lying in this bed, in this room. I tilt my head to get a better look at the book on her nightstand— *Through the Looking-Glass.* She looks like a 1960's-version of Alice, asleep on the floral garden of her sheets, her blond waves of hair, her sky-blue slip, her cat-eye glasses ready to fall from her grasp. I lean forward. "Hey," I say. She stirs at the sound of my voice. I reach out and my hand pushes through the mirror. Just like Alice, I am on the other side. The other side! This weed is stronger than I thought.

"Wake up," I say. She opens her hand, and her glasses fall. I reach for them but grab her arm instead. She opens her eyes and screams a serrated scream. I let go and am back on the bed, am wet with sweat, and the smell of perfume explodes in the room. I get up and check my reflection in the mirror. I look weary, haunted. I walk down the hall and out the door, closing it behind me. The production assistant stands on the landing.

"There you are," he says. "We're ready for you." I follow him to the apartment where they will film the final scene.

"One minute," the costumer says. "The prop master found this today in the garage and thought it would be perfect for you." She opens the box. Inside is a black, sealskin top hat: dented and frayed around the edges. The makeup assistant steps in to powder the humidity of sleep from my face. I place the hat on my head.

"And action," the director calls.

(June 1992)

DEANNA

Deanna is starving. She opens the cupboard and finds a single can of spinach, which she douses with vinegar and eats straight from the can—forkful after forkful, standing at the counter, legs shaking with exhaustion, barely tasting her slapdash dinner. On top of her full-time position in the accounting department at General Electric, she's taken a second job bussing tables part-time at the Ridpath Hotel—anything to pay for the pair of songbird-blue pumps she has on layaway at Mann's. She decides tonight, as she clears another plate filled with half-eaten prime rib and a torn-apart potato, that she will quit this job the moment she makes the final payment on the shoes. She takes the last bite of spinach, rinses her fork, and walks across the hall to brush her teeth. She is too tired to cold cream her face, too tired to put on pajamas; instead she shrugs off her dress, slips under the sheets, and is already falling asleep—lights on, glasses on—when her roommate Gloria pops her head into the room.

"Deanna, can I get back the book I let you borrow? I told Cherry she could read it next, and we're meeting for breakfast tomorrow at Ferguson's." Deanna kicks at the covers. "Don't get up, just tell me where it is," Gloria says.

"Top dresser drawer," says Deanna. Gloria walks to the other side of the bed and pulls on the drawer. It sticks. It's old; like all of the furniture, it came with the apartment. *Completely furnished,* the ad read. Even if the trappings were chipped and decades old, the apartment was perfect for two single girls with few possessions. Gloria pulls harder, and the drawer opens with a screech. Something seems to be stuck on the track. She roots through Deanna's slips and panties until she finds the book.

"Why is it buried?" Gloria asks. *Because I hate the Mad Hatter,* Deanna wants to say. *Because I hate Alice and her deranged looking glass.* Instead, she shrugs. Gloria pulls the book from the drawer.

"You're so strange sometimes," Gloria says. She smooths her nightgown and sits on the edge of the bed.

"Gloria, I can't talk. I'm so tired I could vomit."

"Gee, you don't have to be so dramatic." She gets up in a huff, leaves the book on the bed, slams the door shut. Deanna doesn't like to sleep with the door closed, doesn't like pitch-black rooms, but she is too tired to get up and open it. She sets the forgotten book on the nightstand and turns off the light. Remembers her glasses and pulls them from her face. They do not make it to the nightstand before she falls asleep.

Deanna's eyes aren't closed for five minutes when Gloria pulls on her arm. Hard. Deanna opens her eyes, but it's not Gloria—it's a man. She can make out the outline of his black coattails and trousers.

"Wake up," he says. The moonlight flooding the room illuminates him, but she cannot see his face. She realizes he is standing on the other side of the mirror, and yet his hand is gripping her arm. She screams a shattered glass scream. He lets go, his image fades, and she lies there, fear-frozen. The darkness pins her to the bed, the atmosphere is suddenly thick and oppressive. She can smell sweat and the heady notes of Emeraude rising off her skin and filling the room. Her heart is pounding in her ears; her breath catches in her throat; each tick of the bedside clock is amplified. She peels back the covers, slides onto the floor, crawls the few feet to the door. She reaches up and feels for the doorknob, fumbles with it until it turns. The light from the hallway slices across the floor. She stands and races down the hall, throws open the door to Gloria's room.

"Scoot over," Deanna says.

"You're alive!" says Gloria. "I thought you'd been murdered." She reaches under the covers and squeezes Deanna's hand.

"A nightmare," Deanna says, as she runs her fingers over her arm and feels the welts rising on her skin.

(June 1962)

INGRID & DEANNA

Ingrid pulls the VHS tape from the cardboard slipcase, pops it into the VCR, and sits on the couch next to her mom, Deanna. They are about to watch a modern-day fairy tale filmed in Spokane, the city her mother once called home, the city where she met Ingrid's father, Carl, the city she flew away from and never returned to. Deanna and Ingrid lean toward the TV at the same time, laugh at the same things, but when an apartment appears—Colonial, three stories—Deanna gasps, says, "Pause it!" She turns and shoots Ingrid a look iced with fear. "That," she says, "is my old apartment building. The one where the man in black—" she stops. "You know," she says. Ingrid nods. Of course she knows. It's a story that haunts her. A story she's carried with her for her entire life. It is the reason she doesn't sleep with the doors closed. Doesn't sleep in pitch-black rooms. Doesn't have mirrors in the bedroom. Doesn't like to sleep alone.

(1993)

INGRID

Ingrid meets the actor one September night at a club in Hollywood. He walks in the door with a woman—blonde, paper thin, ethereal. She is the ex-girlfriend of Ingrid's friend, Maurizio. Maurizio swoons over the ex-girlfriend, the ex-girlfriend swoons over Maurizio. The actor and Ingrid are forgotten, unintroduced.

"Hello," the actor says shyly, and then tells her his name. "Hello," Ingrid says shyly, and then tells him her name. He shakes her hand and holds it a beat too long. She does not pull it away. Later, he stands beside her at the bar, but she doesn't know what to say to him, so she stays silent. He stays silent, too. Finally, he sets his beer bottle on the bar, touches her arm, and walks out the door with the Hollywood blonde.

Two years later, after Ingrid has seen his movie, she walks into a San Francisco bookstore with her soon-to-be husband. The actor is in the fiction section with his soon-to-be wife. He stares at Ingrid, Ingrid stares at him. Then Ingrid turns and walks upstairs to the Poetry Room. Ingrid does not read poetry, but the intersection of their lives could be a poem. When she tells her mother about seeing the actor in the bookstore, Deanna's only question is: "Did you ask him if he ever dreamed of us?" It is a question that will go unanswered. It is a question that will haunt Ingrid for decades.

(1994)

◆◆◆◆◆

"Come in," the fortune teller says, and motions for Ingrid to take a seat across from her. Here, in Spokane, in the middle of Riverfront Park, on this hot September day, the cool of the tent is shocking.

"Give me your hands," she says and runs her fingertips over the lines mapping Ingrid's palms.

"There is a man," she says. "Here." She touches the center of Ingrid's left hand. Ingrid laughs.

"Why is this funny?" the woman asks. Her look is pointed, unamused.

"It sounds like a line from a movie," says Ingrid.

"It isn't," the woman says. She shakes her head and continues. "You've crossed paths before." Her fingers stay connected to Ingrid's skin. "Once, twice." The woman leans in for a closer look. "Your past lives here in this city, and also your future. The story of you is repeating—lifetime after lifetime. I see an apartment building. Colonial, three stories. Your story is there. This man's story is there."

"Who is the man?" Ingrid asks.

"Your husband," she says.

"Husband?" Ingrid says. The woman sighs at the interruption.

"A man with dark hair and dark eyes." She looks up at her. "Like yours," she says. "This man," she continues, "left

182

you too soon. Suicide." She runs her finger over another line and stops. "You don't live in Spokane now, do you?" she asks. Ingrid shakes her head. The woman nods. "You will again—someday. The person you once were left and never returned. You will come back—for yourself and for her." Before Ingrid can ask her another question, the woman cuts her off. "That will be ten dollars," she says, and holds out her hand. Ingrid pays and gets up to go. She can feel a headache blooming. The woman takes hold of her arm. "One more thing," she says. "Close your eyes and make a wish." Ingrid does exactly as she says. She finds herself wishing for the man she does not know, from a lifetime that is not hers. Ridiculous, she thinks. A wish for love made by a woman who doesn't believe in it. When she opens her eyes, the fortune teller is staring at her. "That wish," she says, "just set your future into motion." Ingrid shivers, a wave of arctic cold moves up her spine. Then the woman dismisses her with a wave of her hand. Ingrid steps out of the tent. She is dizzy with information. Spots dance before her eyes from the glare of the afternoon sun. She sees a man dressed like Buster Keaton standing on the sidewalk between her and the Looff Carousel. As she walks toward him, he fades to nothing. Intersections of time, she thinks. "Spokane," she says to no one in particular.

(1999)

183

IRIS

Iris stands in front of the dresser mirror, in the guest room, where she has been sleeping since Joseph died. She can't sleep in their bedroom or their bed. It conjures too many memories, too many emotions. One year ago tonight, he took his life. One year ago tonight, her life started to shift and crumble. Earlier in the day, she took herself to a matinee at the Fox Theater to see the newest Buster Keaton picture, but as soon as it was over she remembered what she went there to forget and slipped back into sadness. She dips her fingers into the jar of cold cream and smooths it onto her face. She is tissuing it off when she sees Joseph standing behind her. She turns and finds that she is alone in the room.

"It has to be this maddening heat," she says to herself. "Too hot for June."

When she turns back to the mirror, Joseph is still there. On the other side!

"Iris?" He says her name like a question and then disappears.

INGRID

Ingrid leans in the doorway of the smallest bedroom. The one that was her mother's. There, across from her, exactly as her mother described it, is *the mirror*. She turns to Ivan, whose mother owns the building. Ivan, who invited her to visit after she wrote his family a letter and told them she was writing a book about her mother, about the apartment.

"Has the mirror always been here?" Ingrid asks.

"It was in the apartment when my mom bought the building," he says. "It seemed like it belonged here, so we left it. No one who's rented the apartment seems to mind." Ingrid ponders how this mirror, so seemingly innocent, wedged between the closet and the radiator, could color her mother's nights, and her own, blue-black.

"It's way too hot for a night in June," Ivan says. "How does a scoop of ice cream sound?"

"Huckleberry?" Ingrid asks, then turns and follows him down the hall. She does not see the man who has appeared on the other side of the mirror. The man who is waving to get her attention. The man who is dressed in black.

◆◆◆◆◆

Ingrid calls her mother, Deanna, as soon as she gets back to her room at the Davenport Towers.

"You are not going to believe this!" she says, when her mom says *hello*. "The mirror is still there."

A long silence follows. "And?" her mom says finally.

"It looks so harmless," she says.

"Ingrid—" There's an admonishment in the unfinished sentence.

"Sorry, Mom," she says, before launching into the story of her night. How Ivan arranged a surprise visit to her mom's old apartment. How Ingrid had the feeling she had been there before. Before tonight, before her mother lived there in the 1960s. How it wasn't her mom's story that waited for her in the apartment, but another woman's.

"What do you mean another woman?" her mother asks. "Who is she?"

"I think she was me," Ingrid says.

IRIS

Every night Iris sleeps and dreams of a life not her own. She is herself; the cast of characters are all familiar, but nothing else is. The city is not Spokane, nor are its sounds. Her clothes are unrecognizable, as is her car. If she didn't know better, she'd say she was dreaming the future. She wakes exhausted, day after day. If she told anyone that she feels as if she's living two lives—a daytime life and a nighttime life—they'd think she was mad. Is she? she wonders.

INGRID

Every night Ingrid sleeps and dreams of a life not her own. She is herself; the cast of characters are all familiar, but nothing else is. The city is not Los Angeles, nor are its sounds. Her clothes are unrecognizable, as is her car. If she didn't know better, she'd say she was dreaming the past. She wakes exhausted, day after day. If she told anyone that she feels as if she's living two lives—a daytime life and a nighttime life—they'd think she was mad. Is she? she wonders.

◆◆◆◆◆

Ingrid pieces together Iris's life from the society pages of newspapers in cities Iris called home (Portland, Spokane, Los Angeles, Chicago). Ingrid walks the streets Iris once walked, visits her grave in Portland and leaves stones on her marker, has long conversations with her. Puts flesh onto the bones of her story. When Ingrid can't find a single photo of Iris, she thinks, this is how women are forgotten, erased. She will not let this happen to Iris, so she sits down and starts to write.

IRIS

Iris doesn't believe in marriage, but she says yes to Joseph because she is over twenty-five (*old*, they say, *for a woman to be unwed*) and because he is handsome, because he is kind. After they are married, she resents Joseph for taking her away from the life she lived before she became his wife. After they are married, Iris shows Joseph her hidden self, the one only those closest to her know: the demanding one, the selfish one, the negative one, the one she herself can barely stomach. She waits for him to leave her, and instead, he opens his arms wider and loves her more. After this, she softens and loves him back. They are married—and as happy as two married people can be—until the night he swallows a death sentence of sleeping pills and leaves a note scrawled on a piece of letterhead from Mann's Shoes under the glass of whiskey he uses to wash them down. It reads: "You deserve more."

Following his death, she carries her anger with her like a suitcase as she moves away from their apartment, away from Spokane, and travels the world trying to forget. Finally, the anger mellows to a sadness that is with her until the day she dies. She never remarries.

INGRID

Ingrid believes in one-night stands, the way other women believe in love. One-night stands are safe. One-night stands do not interrupt her life. One-night stands do not have the power to destroy her. In spite of this, Ingrid has a memory of love that she carries inside of her. The problem is, she doesn't know whose memory it is because it is not hers.

IRIS

Iris calls a taxi to take her to the train station, and then calls the apartment's caretaker, George, to carry her bags downstairs. She stands in the middle of the living room and takes one last look around; her memories swell and crash into each other. "I'll miss you," she says to the apartment, "but I can't spend one more night here. It's time to go." There is a knock on the front door. It's George. As always, he stands in the doorway and makes small talk for too long—about the weather, the local news, other tenants in the building.

Outside, the taxi honks its horn.

"We better get downstairs or I'll miss my train." Iris says.

"But what about all the furniture?" he says motioning around the apartment.

"Do with it what you will," she says. "I'm traveling light."

"Light?" he says as he casts an eye over her stack of suitcases, her trunk. She follows his glance and laughs.

"Where're you heading, Mrs. Mann?"

"The Ravenswood Apartments. Los Angeles, California."

INGRID

One September Tuesday, Ingrid's agent calls to tell her that her novel has sold at auction. The amount shocks, makes her dizzy. She congratulates Ingrid, tells her a celebration is in order.

"Treat yourself," she says.

Ingrid calls Ivan to tell him that soon the apartment building will be famous. He congratulates her, tells her a celebration is in order.

"Eat cake," he says. "Drink champagne."

Then he tells her that he has a surprise for her. "The apartment where your mom, and Iris, lived will be vacant by the end of the month. It's yours if you want it. What do you say?"

"I say, 'Goodbye, Los Angeles. Hello, Spokane!'"

◆◆◆◆◆

When Ingrid moves into the apartment, she leaves the mirror propped up against the wall in what was once her mom's bedroom. At first she keeps it covered, then she uncovers it. At first she keeps the door closed, then she keeps it open. She asks Ivan to move the mirror to the garage, then she asks him to move it back in. The room remains empty until she buys a writing desk, a lamp, a chair. Later, she buys a jade plant and moves in her books. She calls it her writing room, but she only writes at night, and she does not go into the room after dark. She keeps the myth of the mirror alive, but she has no experiences of her own with the man in black. She types drafts of her new novel on a vintage, ocean-blue Underwood typewriter that lives on the table in the dining room. She calls it *Spokane Wonderland*.

INGRID & THE ACTOR

Ingrid sits in the Peacock Room of the Davenport Hotel waiting for the actor whose production company has optioned her novel. It's happy hour, and the bar is crowded with tourists and business people. She realizes her mistake in suggesting they meet here. She orders a glass of wine.

"Red," she says. "Anything local."

"Make that two," a man says, and slips into the chair beside her. The voice famous, unmistakable. Unchanged in the thirty years since they first met. They are both older now, slanting into sixty. Sixty, she thinks. It feels impossible. She turns to face him. He extends his hand, says his name, "Jack." She takes his hand and says her name, "Ingrid." At first they talk about small things: the weather, what they're reading, what they're watching. Then he deep dives into their shared project: his vision, hers. How to recreate the locations that no longer exist, who to cast. She has a hard time following the conversation, because all she really wants to know is: *Did you ever dream about my mom? Iris? Me?* A server passes with a slice of cake. It's stacked, seamed with huckleberry. Ingrid stares at it a beat too long. She has a flash of memory that is not hers. He takes her confusion for want.

"Hungry?" he asks. She laughs. "Starving," she says. He orders more food than they will eat, another round.

After the hamburgers, the French fries, the second glass of wine, she reminds him that they met once, in a bar in Hollywood, then crossed paths again at a bookstore in San Francisco. "I remember," he says. "The King King, right? City Lights?" She nods.

"A lifetime ago," she says.

"A lifetime," he says.

"And now here we are," says Ingrid. "Strange isn't it?"

"Not so strange," Jack says. "Considering." He reaches into the inside pocket of his coat, slides a vintage photo card face down across the bar. She picks it up and reads the back: *Joseph and Iris Mann. September 19, 1914.*

"How?" she asks, shocked. "Where? I've never been able to find a photo of her."

He smiles his shy smile. "At Mt. Vernon, when we were filming." He reaches out to tuck a fallen strand of hair behind her ear. A woman says his name and lifts her phone. The flash blinds. Ingrid blinks until the afterglow stops. She turns the photo over. She sees Jack's face, she sees her own. She bites her lip to keep from crying. Before she can say anything, he raises his glass.

"To lifetimes," he says.

(2022)

Interlude: Ingrid

Ingrid walks into the gallery in downtown Los Angeles. The room is filled with a cluster of celebrities and art acolytes. The exhibit is called "Wonderland." She plucks a plastic cup filled with cheap red wine from the tray of a server circling the room.
"What do you think?" It's Jack who asks, the paintings are his. All large-scale, all color-saturated. Inspired, according to the gallery sheet, by Alice in Wonderland and a recurring dream the artist has had for decades. "Is this an homage to Alice's madness or your own?" she says and laughs. "Walk with me," Jack says, and holds out his hand. They view the exhibit in reverse, from the newest painting to the oldest: the Cheshire Cat asleep in a maple tree in front of Mt. Vernon Apartments; Tweedle Dee and Tweedle Dum fighting on the train tracks, the Steam Plant's twin stacks looming in the background; the White Rabbit buying a watch at Dodson's Jewelers; the Queen of Hearts eating pie at Cyrus O'Leary's; the Mad Hatter sitting atop the Great Northern clocktower—its hands twinned at twelve. Thirty minutes later they are standing in front of the final painting, the first in the series. It is a 1960s version of Alice asleep on the floral garden of her sheets. Ingrid sees blond waves of hair, a sky-blue slip, cat-eye glasses about to fall from her grasp. In the right corner, Jack's signature and the date—1992. Alice's face is her mother's.

(2024)

Postlude: The Apartment

The strange, beautiful stories of life are
forever circling,
forever skipping and tumbling through time,
forever repeating,
forever waiting to be heard.
Are you listening?

Dear Reader,

Many have asked if Mt. Vernon Apartments actually exist? The answer is a resounding yes.

An advertisement for Mt. Vernon in the September 1, 1916 edition of the *Spokesman Review* declares it "Spokane's Most Modern Apartment." The ad guarantees a Hughes Electric Range in every kitchen, as well as a secondary, small-print promise that the stove "insures kitchen happiness in this splendid new apartment." A lovely token, not to the renters but to the maids, which most of the early residents employed. The advertisement goes on to describe the apartment in delightful detail: *This high-class apartment, built by the architect and owner, O.M. Lilliquist, has seven apartments of six rooms each. It is a typical twentieth century home for those who demand the uttermost in convenience and economy. Each apartment is complete with large front porch, spacious lawn, combination sun and sleeping room, heavy oak floors, fireplace, every latest built-in feature, all-electric kitchen, with cooler. A private garage for each apartment also.*

In the beginning, Mt. Vernon was home to the city's movers and shakers and their leisured wives, and then later to secretaries and shopgirls and salesmen, and later still to painters and poets, students and single moms. This book is my valentine to them and to the people of Spokane. To note, I have added three additional apartments to the original seven, given Clementine's kitchen a gas stove (my apologies to the ultra-coveted Hughes Electric Range), and placed Iris and Joseph Mann at Mt. Vernon in 1914, two years before it was built. While I've set these stories in and around the very real city of Spokane, I've fictionalized the lives of the tenants. Any similarities to those living or dead is purely coincidental, except when it's not.

As far as the rumors that have begun to swirl, I can tell you this: a movie may or may not have been filmed at Mt. Vernon; my mother may or may not have lived in an apartment on the second floor; a certain bygone Spokane socialite may or may not have called the place home; and a doll named Willie may or may not have spent decades face down in the laundry room rafters, placed there by someone who may or may not be famous.

Just know, whether the gossip is true or false, Mt. Vernon is indeed a magical place.

With love, Carla

PS As for the 1914 photograph at the Davenport Hotel, that may or may not include this writer, you'll have to find it and decide for yourself.

Acknowledgements

First and foremost, this collection would not exist without the love and support of Jeanne and Eddy Tanaka. One million mahalos for opening your hearts and the doors of Mt. Vernon to me. Thank you to Bruce Rutledge, Justine Chan, and Adriana Campoy at Chin Music Press for believing in me and my stories. To Tiffany Aldrich MacBain for her gentle, intelligent edits. To the literary journals who published early versions of these stories: *The Ana*, *Ricepaper*, and *Crazyhorse*. To the Joel E. Ferris Research Archives at the Northwest Museum of Arts and Culture for providing the photographs that inspired each story in this collection, and to Alex Fergus for going above and beyond with his archival aid. To my IAIA family, especially Jon Davis who said yes to my application and in doing so changed my world.

And a heartfelt thank you to all who were there with me as I wrote and fretted and fretted and wrote. Brandon Hobson for your friendship, and for always lending a literary hand. JD forever. Kate Peterson, my literary champion, and favorite person to drink wine with in haunted Spokane speakeasies. Toni Jensen for seeing the fairy tales hidden in my work before I did, and for your infinite kindness. Marie-Helene Bertino, yours was the voice I heard while writing. Ramona Ausubel, *Old Ladies 4eva*—even if I have to stand here alone in my big glasses and satin jacket and wait another decade or so for you to catch up. Derek Palacio for being the best den dad to his pack of writerly she-wolves. Tommy Orange for the inspiration and the laughter. Joe Holt for your advice, encouragement, and photos of Bandit "Danger" Holt. Darien Hsu Gee, literary map maker and guide. Kristin Alkire for always thinking I am the coolest person in the room, when we both know I'm not. Kelli Estes, my dear friend with the biggest heart and the kindest words. Chelsea Hicks for forging the path. Lanas forever. Kristiana Kahakauwila for answering my island call, "Let's go kaukau!" Zoe, Dom, and Cheyenne for Seattle. Kasia Merrill, my writing wife and sweetest of all hearts: Chinatown grandma ghosts and mooncakes forever and ever. Richard Beaman for being the Laura to my Nellie until the end of time. My darling Clementine for sharing the fairy tale of your life with me. Spokane for your strangeness, your stories, and our tangled history. Auntie Debbie for starting me on my witchy path. Bob for (over)feeding me while I wrote this collection. To quote Sophia, "Everything you see I owe to spaghetti." My family—Mom, Kai, Dana, Cristen, Kevin, Steven, Laurelle, Carl, Ethan, Jacob, and Pip—for the food, the love, and the laughter. My dad, who is eating Chinese food 24/7 in the celestial heavens (which I imagine is far better than the one the non-eaters have to go to). And last but never least, my lifelong idol, Auntie Helen (if there is a disco in the afterlife, she is there).

Carla Crujido is the Nonfiction Editor at *River Styx Magazine.*
She holds an MFA in Creative Writing from the Institute of
American Indian Arts and has had work published in *Crazyhorse,*
*Yellow Medicine Review, Ricepaper Magazine, Tinfish Press, The
Ana,* and elsewhere. She lives in the Pacific Northwest.

carlacrujido.com | @carlacrujido